# Contemporary Macedonian Fiction

# CONTEMPORARY MACEDONIAN FICTION

Translated and Edited by Paul Filev

**DALKEY ARCHIVE PRESS**
McLean, IL / Dublin

Library of Congress Cataloging-in-Publication Data
Names: Filev, Paul, translator.
Title: Contemporary macedonian fiction / edited and translated by Paul Filev.
Description: First edition. | McLean, IL : Dalkey Archive, 2019. | Includes bibliographical references and index.
Identifiers: LCCN 2018026124 | ISBN 9781628972818 (pbk. : acid-free paper)
Subjects: LCSH: Short stories, Macedonian--Translations into English. | Macedonian fiction--21st century. | Macedonian fiction--20th century.
Classification: LCC PG1194 .C63 2018 | DDC 891.8/193--dc23
LC record available at https://lccn.loc.gov/2018026124

This book is partially funded by the Ministry of Culture of the Republic of Macedonia

www.dalkeyarchive.com
McLean, IL / Dublin

Printed on permanent/durable acid-free paper.

# Contents

# INTRODUCTION

THERE IS MUCH to recommend from the modest but growing body of Macedonian literary works. However, the small number of translations available in English has made the task of connecting others to Macedonian literature difficult. The aim of this anthology is to make available to readers a selection of some of the most exciting and innovative contemporary works of short fiction from Macedonia.

Here it is important to make mention of two previous anthologies that introduced Macedonian writing to English speakers: *The Big Horse and Other Stories of Modern Macedonia* (1974, ed. by Milne Holton) and *Change of the System: Stories of Contemporary Macedonia* (2000, ed. by Richard Gaughran and Zoran Ančevski). Broadly speaking, each work encompasses a particular period of Macedonian literary history, and both works follow the evolution of Macedonian short fiction that began in the second half of the twentieth century. The first period dates from 1945 when the Macedonian language was standardized, and relates to literature written in the post-World War II period. Stories from this period—collected in the former anthology—are characterized by more traditional styles of writing. The second period dates from the establishment of the Republic of Macedonia as a sovereign state in 1991, and can be described as the "post-independence" period of literary expression that lasted to the turn of the millennium. As demonstrated in the latter collection, stories from this period are marked by a shift from realist to postmodernist narrative techniques.

This anthology continues the project of making the work of Macedonian writers available to a wider audience. It follows the turbulent second period that marked the first ten years of Macedonian statehood from 1991 to 2001. All but one of the stories included here—displaying a plurality of styles—were written in the first two decades of the twenty-first century. This period can be characterized as a "post-transition" period—but one that is still not distinguished by a sense of "arrival," "settledness," or "stability." Instead, these remain elusive features in Macedonian society to which the stories from this period attest.

The anthology is an eclectic mix and—like any selection—the sixteen stories chosen were based on subjective considerations. No anthology of this length could be considered a representative cross section of the Macedonian short story. Nor is it an authoritative compendium. To those familiar with the literary scene in Macedonia, omissions from this anthology will be obvious. Despite being just a sampling, the stories chosen for this collection offer a broad range of contemporary Macedonian prose intended for a general audience.

The problem of choice is a dilemma all too familiar to the translator. Like a word-puzzle enthusiast poring over clues—only ones that aren't deliberately misleading—the literary translator may spend hours, days, sometimes weeks (for the most part happily) deciding on a word or phrase that will properly convey the sense of the original. And not just words, but also sentence structure, level of formality, punctuation, sometimes even spelling.

In my translations of the stories collected here, I have generally remained faithful to the originals when possible, though considerations of English style had to be taken into account. Long, run-on sentences are often found in Macedonian literary texts, but modern English style prefers shorter sentences and a more sparing use of multiple subordinate clauses. Thus, while attempting to render the sense of the original, I looked for ways to keep the language clear without compromising the writer's style.

These stories range from the surreal to the mundane, from reality to fantastic situations, from comedy to pathos, or a mixture of both. Bert Stein's "Seventh Son of a Seventh Son," which blends elements of popular culture and personal experience into an affecting account of events before and after the collapse of Yugoslavia, is the only overtly political text in this anthology. However, the cultural and political backdrop against which the writers penned their stories—the past decade in Macedonia having been marked by authoritarianism, instability, and corruption—perhaps speaks to the recurring themes within these stories.

The overall sense is one of a world gone askew. In Tomislav Osmanli's comic satire "Strained," a politico-businessman who's had a bellyful of work and the stress of his position swallows his own computer and is treated by a doctor for an obstructed bowel. The doctor wonders if this unusual case isn't just symptomatic of a wider malaise—or, to put it more crudely, of a world that's gone to crap. Similarly, the title character in Jagoda Mihajlovska-Georgieva's "Imrul from the Beach," a jaded and disillusioned economic migrant comes to the painful realization about his own complicity in the bizarre and desperate situation he finds himself in: a stranger in a strange land, peddling useless gadgets to uninterested beach tourists.

The stories are permeated with strange events, inexplicable happenings, and unusual characters. The protagonist of Mitko Madžunkov's enigmatic story "Rods" searches for something that will give meaning to his own life and at the same time has universal importance: these are the mysterious "rods" that are kept hidden in the soil. Despite his uncertainty about these rods, he digs them up daily in order to check on their condition. And though assured of their existence, he and his tribe constantly—and it might be said neurotically—persist in verifying their reality, seeking to confirm the validity of their own lives. While in Blaže Minevski's "Dirt," an aching meditation on the need to preserve memory, the unnamed narrator searches for a way to make sense and create meaning from loss. As he sits for a painting in the vestibule of a church, he recounts the story of the mysterious disappearance of his little brother, who liked to eat dirt. "Only time that is remembered belongs to us," he says to the friend who is painting the event being recounted to him.

"After you sign your name beneath the painting, I too will never forget what happened back then." And in Nenad Joldeski's "My Mother, the Flood, and the Short Story," the literary devices of the "lost" manuscript, of false authorship, and of the frame story are employed to great effect. A mother confronts her son with her suspicion that her husband—his father—stole her "missing" stories. Soon after, the father seeks out the son's opinion on a "new" story he claims to have written. In just a few pages, Joldeski manages to build tension surrounding the mystery of the authorship. Embedded within the main narrative is the story that is purportedly written by the father, which heightens the tension. The extravagant phenomena and events in this story—such as the room filled with web-like strings of words that have left all the books blank—create an atmosphere of doubt and apprehension that underscore the theme of the uncertainty of provenance.

Alienation is a pervasive theme in this volume. Frustration, futility, and absurdity are all seen as inescapable features of modern life. Driven to distraction in his quest to retrieve his ATM card, which has been "swallowed" by a machine, the protagonist of Dragi Mihajlovski's "A Slip of Paper" wonders if anything much has changed since the days of socialism, when completing even the most basic task was dependent on the arbitrary whim of state officials rather than on nominal procedures. Faced with absurd obstacles at every attempt to get his card back, he questions whether he should have resorted to the old ways of doing things: "Perhaps I should have told her that I work in the neighborhood, that I'm a professor at the university nearby, that I'm in a hurry, that . . . But my mouth remained closed and I didn't say anything. I wanted to go through the procedure routinely, without resorting to connections. I was their old customer, but these were different times. Capitalism had arrived. We had a more modern state now, which we loved because it was ours, the Republic of Macedonia." Despite the arrival of capitalism and the modern state, in the end he is left with the bitter realization that one still has to endure all sorts of nonsense, that things "don't just work," that "no one cares," that an attempt to beat a path of sense through all the absurdity is futile.

In fact, most of the protagonists in the stories come to some sort of bitter realization about their lives—but not always with resignation. The women in Elizabeta Bakovska's "The Yasnaya Polyana File," Rumena Bužarovska's "Lily," and Marta Markoska's "The Heights of Felicity" have all learned to suppress their feelings and to make compromises in their relationships with the men in their lives—in some cases with tragic and fatal consequences. But ultimately, in their own way, each of the women refuses to succumb to despair. With a mixture of pathos and wit, these stories trace the transition of the women from disillusionment to provocation, rebellion, and even reckoning. Bitter experience, however, is not restricted to the adult world. Narrated by a child, Snežana Mladenovska Angjelkov's "Menka" recounts the story of how a young girl's childish prank—provoked by a neighborhood bully and his intimidating mother—backfires and leaves her with the sour, bitter reality of a harsh and despotic world. Though softened by local color and peppered with an assortment of bizarre characters, Mladenovska Angjelkov's story is an unflinching, unromantic portrait of small-town life.

At times the texts mirror the protagonist's state of ambivalence, anxiety, and uncertainty. The stories by Olivera Ќorveziroska, Aleksandar Prokopiev, and Sasho Dimoski dispense with traditional elements of narrative, and sometimes even with punctuation, employing postmodern narrative techniques—fragmentation, discontinuity, ambiguity, play, irony—to problematize the relationship between language and reality. "Language needs to be restrained from head to toe, because one can never be sure whether it might escape us (or assail us): it escapes/assails us from all sides, it must be harnessed at both ends until we find it of use, until we want it to serve us," states the narrator of Olivera Ќorveziroska's "The Irreplaceable," a playful but melancholy story that explores the insufficiency of language to express the loss of a loved one. While in Aleksandar Prokopiev's "Fragmente Meiner Mutter," fragmentation of the text—alluded to in the title—mirrors the protagonist's contradictory and mutually undermining relationship with his mother. The protagonist is a painter, and, like the canvases he paints that "consistently emphasize the dichotomy of real/unreal," his complex relationship with his mother emphasizes the destabilizing absence of any certainties. Sasho Dimoski's "Simon," on the other hand, reads almost like a prose poem that begs to be read out loud. It's an intense, feverish, and somewhat surreal account narrated from the perspective of a woman standing beside the disciple Simon when he becomes the Apostle Peter. From the gospels, we know that Simon, whose name means "listen," was not always as stable and reliable as his name suggests. After appointing him his apostle, Jesus changed Simon's name to Peter, meaning "rock"—the rock on which he would build his church—altering Simon's very identity, one might say, from his previous self, impulsive and volatile. The story's postmodern concerns with instability and identity are emphasized through the narrator's passionate and repeated appeals to "the impulsive and volatile" Simon. The narrator places the importance of love—which knows only the soul and clings not to the body— above the arbitrariness of names: "Listen to me! Listen to me! . . . Stay, Simon, stay. I'll call you by whatever name you desire. Choose your own name, just stay. Fine then, perhaps Peter. You can call yourself whatever you like. We'll even invent other stories together. Just stay."

Unable to adapt to their circumstances in a largely hostile and unstable environment, some protagonists lose all hope of making sense of the world. They have either become or else are on their way to becoming complete psychological wrecks. In Žarko Kujundžiski's "Story Addict," the pervasive distress and disorientation of the protagonist have grown to the point where he has lost all sense of reason. His insatiable and uncontrollable craving for stories and his dread of running out of them has led him to commit desperate acts. These include smashing bookshop windows and reading people's mail. Ordered by the authorities to remain indoors, he pleads his case: "Apparently I pose a danger to the community. Apparently I peer through people's windows, I listen in on them, I open their mail, I stick my nose into people's personal business. They treat me like a criminal. And all I do is just read and listen to stories. Is there anything wrong with that?

I'm an ordinary reader. I'm not a thief, a thief of stories." The story ends with three news reports that leave open the question of his complicity and of his sanity. For the protagonist of Kalina Maleska's "The Nonhuman Adversary," however, the buildup to the tipping point is gradual. One day, Miron Aronievski—an otherwise capable and proficient translator—becomes locked in battle with an ever-expanding text he is translating. At every attempt to complete the translation, the document increases by another page. Determined not to be outmaneuvered, Miron dives into the document itself through a portal in the computer screen, desperate to reach the end of the text.

It is always a pleasure to recommend stories and share them with others. The reader who wanders through the thought-provoking stories collected here will be impressed by the quality and breadth of writing styles in the works of Macedonian writers. The reader will gain insight into contemporary Macedonian literature, and it is hoped that he or she will be inspired to continue exploring Macedonian fiction in translation.

*

My deep gratitude goes to the following for their editorial assistance, encouragement, and advice, without which this anthology may not have come to fruition: John O'Brien, Alex Andriesse, Victor Friedman, Christina Kramer, Rumena Bužarovska, Julie Stafford, Alicia Filev, and special thanks to my chess partner Jim for his inspiration and tireless support.

Paul Filev
July 2017

# Contemporary Macedonian Fiction

Translated and Edited by Paul Filev

# MITKO MADŽUNKOV

## *Rods*

HAVE YOU HEARD of the rods? You've no idea how miraculous they are? Well, to be honest, the same goes for me. But my mental image of them has always been unusually clear. I don't know what they are or what they stand for, but what I do know is that they exist and that they're important. I also know that some of the rods are my personal property.

I distinctly remember the continued importance of the rods. We had to dig them up every day to make sure they were where they were supposed to be. On my first dig, not only did I get a good look at them—although at the time my understanding of their role in the constitution of the world was pretty hazy—but I recognized them immediately, like the echo of a word heard long ago, an important word: Aha, I said to myself, so that's what the rods are!

To be honest, the word "rod" had never meant much to me. It seems I was never even sure of its basic meaning. For instance, it never crossed my mind that the word also refers to a stick, and even a shoot. Originally, I thought the meaning of the word had to do with a fishing pole, or with the beams used as buttresses for the support of dams and other structures. Its predominant meaning—clearly figurative—had to do with a type of cartilaginous bony growth in the lower region of the spine. In any case, even without ascertaining its meaning, it was clear to me that the

3

word "rod" was of an extremely dubious etymology. Deep down I knew that when someone said, "I've got rods," they weren't complaining of illness, but rather they were recklessly revealing an important secret.

The rods were hidden in the soil. To make sure they were intact, one had to dig. The hole typically resembled a freshly dug grave carved out neatly in the fertile red loam. Strangely enough, the rods weren't lying at the bottom of the "grave." Instead, they were hovering freely in the middle of it, like bones in a coffin. Because of this, the digging didn't stop when the rods were encountered, but rather when they remained hovering in the middle of the void.

The rods' appearance didn't surprise me. They were in a box, arranged like sticks of dynamite or a dozen yellow candles. On first inspection, the digger (eventually me), stripped to the waist, merely glanced at them, and said that everything looked to be in order (I supposed he meant that they were dry).

Neither then nor later did I discover the meaning hidden behind this daily ritual. The hole-cum-grave concealed something precious to us that could easily spoil, and that's why a daily inspection was required. At the same time, it seemed to me that the risk of damaging the rods in the very act of digging far outweighed the benefit of having to check on them. Couldn't we just assume that they were safe for at least one week? Or until the first rain? No one would even entertain such a thought. The daily monitoring of the rods was more important than anything else. The task was not unlike checking our own pulse, to see if we were still alive.

That probably explains the unusual tension that was part and parcel of the digging. How else can one account for the barely hidden fear, masked by typical banter and routine tasks, with which the appearance of the rods was awaited? It seems to me that the arduous nature of the work itself aided us in maintaining our equilibrium. But behind the sweat on our naked torsos, and in the depths of our eyes, there remained just one question— especially when we were in the middle of digging: What if the rods aren't in their correct place? However, I never dared to ask myself that question. Nor did it become clear to me what might happen to the rods. What if they got wet? Fine, that wasn't out of the question. But then why did this fear remain even during dry periods, when there was no chance of a drop of moisture penetrating the baked earth? Clearly, the rods were threatened from all sides (and with them, naturally, so were we).

What troubled me most wasn't the thought that the rods might disappear from their proper place, but instead that they might sink to the bottom of the grave (as I unconsciously referred to the hole). This increased my fear, all the more so because, were that to happen, it would double our suffering. If I don't find the rods in the middle of the "grave," will they instead be at the bottom? In that event, they will certainly no longer be "intact." The fact that they were no longer suspended in midair would indicate that they'd already spoiled and were possibly "defunct." But there should still be some visible remnants. Yet what if the remnants disappeared altogether? Such thoughts—like fear itself—were simply not allowed.

It became clear to me that the rods were some kind of totem belonging to the whole tribe. We had to hide them well and keep them safe. We had to check up on them. But we couldn't be certain that they would last forever.

No one was even permitted a sideways glance at them. During digging, if any strangers happened along, the whole tribe would paint their faces and begin their rowdy pursuits, if only to somehow distract the uninvited guests from our holy rods.

Although their resemblance to dynamite gave rise to some suspicion, over time I became increasingly convinced that the rods were actually the seeds of nature, from which grow not only the trees for beams and fishing poles, but also life itself, with all its joys and sorrows. Strangely, as time passed and my digging slowed, the fear that the rods had spoiled, or sunk to the bottom of the "grave," or even completely disappeared, dissipated. So much so that gradually I forgot that fear, as if it had just vanished.

By then I was completely exhausted from almost continuous digging. I spent the daylight hours attempting to get to the rods (in wintertime it wasn't so easy), while at night under the cover of darkness, I burrowed fearlessly down into the depths of the hole that served as a hiding place in which to rest. So it remains to this day. Although I don't expect that you'll believe me, I'm certain, now, that at the bottom of that hole I'll never find any spoiled and defunct remains. And I'm just as certain that the rods—among which are my own, like faded bones—will never stop hovering in the middle of the void, like a sky from which life will spring eternal and be forever renewed. Life, which is capable of stemming the mightiest of floods, sailing the sparkling seas, and enduring the pain of its own soul, like a bony growth hidden in the lower region of the spine, which is called the cross.

# DRAGI MIHAJLOVSKI

## *A Slip of Paper*

I ALMOST WENT crazy practically first thing that morning. It was a Monday, and if things go wrong on a Monday, they say your whole week will be topsy-turvy, from start to finish. Whatever rotten establishment I entered, I was forced to fill out a slip of paper, some sort of form. Two Mondays in three weeks when nothing went right for me. I put up with about as much as I could, but, believe you me, I'd had enough! Some sort of black magic was involved. Against my better judgment, I began to believe there were supernatural forces at work, and the whole time I felt an almost constant urge to jump out of my skin and return to it on a more agreeable day.

As I've already said, things went wrong for me practically first thing that Monday morning. Barely awake, I went to the ATM at the Commercial Bank here in Radišani to withdraw some cash, in case it came in handy for shopping, or even at the post office (imagine it, at the post office here they told me they don't accept cards, as if you're helping yourself to what's theirs with a card that, in their view, isn't money!). But something wasn't working right, and rather than assuming I might have typed in the wrong PIN number (they'd changed it at the bank a few days before that, and in a somewhat careless and flippant manner, qualities bestowed upon me by God, I said something rude to them, but they were used to such things and ignored my carrying on about

7

it, although, when I think about it now, I was in the right; I
didn't want them to change my PIN number at all, or anything
else for that matter, because then I would make silly mistakes,
you know, like being forgetful, and so on, and it really bugged
me that we've gradually been turned into numbers, not to mention approaching old age goes hand in hand with forgetfulness!),
like a fool I stabbed at the keypad again.

Even in my morning madness I was convinced that the
machine was wrong (which isn't true, a machine is never, or
*almost* never, wrong), and I stubbornly persisted in typing in
the wrong PIN number that was stuck in my mind as being the
correct one. As you would expect, after the third attempt, the
ATM swallowed my card, abandoning me to my fate.

When I realized that I was left without that indispensable
card, I took out my wallet, in which I'd stored the correct PIN
number that I'd assumed I knew by heart, but clearly didn't.
Why was that so frustrating? Probably a legacy of living in what
used to be Yugoslavia, where going to the bank was an ordeal
that would cause you to break out into a cold sweat, living in
fear of having made an error or there being inaccuracies in your
papers! Now, a hundred feet from the ATM, I knew the PIN
number perfectly, but it was too late. I took off immediately to
the bank branch in Čair in the hope that one of the tellers there
could help. I'd been a customer of theirs for many years (I was
even older than the bank itself, and I remember clearly when it
split from the Stopanska Bank, and we automatically became its
customers), but nothing helped. The female teller just gave me
a pitiful look from behind the counter, and said:

"Ah, ah!"

"What does 'ah, ah!' mean?"

"It means you have to wait at least two weeks before you can
get your card back," she said.

"I beg your pardon?" I said with astonishment. "You mean
to say it takes two weeks for an ordinary card to be sent from
Radišani to the main branch?"

"We have to wait for pension day," she explained firmly,

"that's when the ATMs are opened up and refilled. After that, they'll find your card and take it back to the main branch!"

I thanked the kind bank teller—what else could I do?—and went back home.

Two weeks later I went to the main branch, which had also been relocated. It was now in downtown Skopje, and not on "that" side of the Vardar River. Happy and relieved that I would finally get my card back, after having somehow made it through two weeks without it, I pressed the buzzer and entered the tall building. Inside there were porters, security guards, bank tellers, all of whom just look you up and down as if you've come to rob the stupid place, instead of to collect your damned card just so you can live—incidentally, a card that they live off too by charging exorbitantly high fees.

"Yep?" the female teller, a real backwoods type, addressed me informally. She reeked of cheap perfume and her political party affiliations.

"Well now, you see, about two weeks ago—" I began my account and, for some unknown reason, caught myself acting the part of a real hick.

"Other building." The bumpkin cut me off, and literally waved me away, pointing to the exit. As if she cared one way or another whether I was a hick or not.

I followed her orders—what else could I do, I ask you? I went outside, walked down the street a bit more, and almost smack up against the building from which I'd just emerged, there was another tall building with the same sign. "This must be it!" I said to myself, and entered it after passing through all the security measures carried out by authorized personnel. Above several of the counters was a sign clearly displaying the word "CARDS." I stood in the line and waited. I was soon called. They offered me a seat (like they do in the West no less!), and, after thoroughly checking me out, the female teller asked me what kind of problem I had.

"All kinds," I attempted a little joke, but she just looked at me sourly as if to say, if this is just a joke, then go and joke

somewhere else, not here, and I returned my expression to its
original cold and impassive form, and told her what happened
to me two weeks ago in Radišani.

"ID card!" she ordered, and pulled her sharp gaze away from me.

"Here you are," I said, handing her the ID card, which was
virtually already out of my wallet.

She disappeared for a while, and when she returned, she said,
almost angrily: "Hand me the slip!"

"What slip?" I said, puzzled. I almost jumped out of my
skin because I was convinced she had nothing on me, that I was
carrying all the other necessary documents: ID card, driver's
license, passport.

"The slip of paper from the bank where your card was taken!"
she said, almost hostilely. "You must've gone inside the branch,
asked for your card, and were given a slip!"

"But, my good lady," I said—and she was about as much of
a lady as my great-grandmother, who carried loaves of bread in
a sack on her back when she came home to her village from the
market at night—"there's no bank in Radišani! Just an ATM
stuck on a wall, and a broken sign that says 'Bank Soon.' The
technicians in the shop behind the wall told me they had nothing to do with the ATM, and that I had to speak to someone
here at the main branch. I'm at the right place, aren't I?" I said,
admittedly feigning naïveté.

"Here," she said, and tossed me my ID card, "come back after
3:00 p.m.," and she looked away from me, giving me a sign to
get up and leave so the person after me could take my place.

Fool that I am, I got up and did as I was told. I behaved as if
this wasn't even a privatized bank, as if it were still the old socialist times when we had just one or two banks that were under
strict government control. The staff in those two lovely buildings
also behaved the same way, as if they were still living in those
times when bank tellers were like gods, and anyone who wanted
to get something from the bank had to wait for hours, staring
at the clock to make sure the time to go home hadn't arrived,
meaning they'd have to return the following day to repeat the
whole thing over again. But it was different now. At least that's

what it seemed like to me. Banks had cropped up all over the place, but most of us, clearly out of habit, kept banking at the old Commercial Bank!

At home I explained what had happened, turning the incident around slightly to my own advantage. But I was easy to read, my weary expression a dead giveaway, so I recounted the whole experience in detail from the beginning.

"Did they mean the slip of paper they gave you at the bank branch at the university?" said my daughter.

"There was nothing on it," said my wife. "It was just a scrap of paper. I threw it out!"

"That's all you ever do—throw things out," I said, barely waiting for the chance to launch into an argument so I could feel some relief, so I could take some of the heat off me, shrug them off, and enjoy what was left of the bad day that could have happened to anyone.

"Go on, try and remember," said my daughter, looking at us both reproachfully. "Didn't you just say that when you went there you were given something to fill out?"

"Yes, yes," I said, and recalled that that had been the case. "After those crazy Monday mornings two weeks ago, I remembered that I could take out some money with my passbook," I said.

"And?" said my wife, seething from the needless insult I'd inflicted on her, and waiting for just the right moment to let me have it.

"From downtown, I set off on foot to the bank branch at our university, and I went in, alone, there was no one else in there. I said good morning. I gave the teller the withdrawal slip and my ID card and told her how much money I wanted to withdraw. I wasn't in the red, so I knew there shouldn't be any problem. 'Is that all?' the teller said, glancing at my ID card, and giving me a sharp look. 'That's all,' I said quickly in a very hoarse and weak voice.

"I thought the transaction was complete and that everything was in order after she counted the money twice, once by hand and again through the electronic banknote counter beside her, but I was wrong. 'Fill out the slip,' she said and handed me some sort of two-page document. 'A mere formality, but we have to have your details with us as our customer.' 'But I've already filled out one of these slips before and left it at the branch in Čair. I always do my banking there, but now, because I've had to, I've come here to you for the first time!'

"'It won't kill you to fill it out again,' she said to me, and began tapping my money, which she was holding in her hands enticingly on the counter.

"'Please,' I said more affably, and that image of old socialist Yugoslavia came back to me while beads of sweat broke out on my forehead, 'would you mind filling it out for me? I don't have my glasses with me.'

"Perhaps I should have told her that I work in the neighborhood, that I'm a professor at the university nearby, that I'm in a hurry, that . . . But my mouth remained closed and I didn't say anything. I wanted to go through the procedure routinely, without resorting to connections. I was their old customer, but these were different times. Capitalism had arrived. We had a more modern state now, which we loved because it was ours, the Republic of Macedonia . . .

"'No, it's not possible,' she said, 'either do it now or come back for the money tomorrow with the slip of paper filled out!'

"'So that means . . .?' was all I said.

"'You heard me,' she said almost shouting, 'there are no hidden meanings here. Fill it out and come back tomorrow. And that's final!' I grabbed the slip, scrunched it up, and, in a furious sweat, rushed out through the familiar security exit.

"'See that. Do you see that?' I heard behind me, 'when it comes to filling out forms, they make out as if they're blind! Well, I won't do the work for them . . .' I couldn't stand it any longer. I went off feeling awkward, almost bent out of shape, and took a cab with the last bit of my cash—without leaving a tip for the driver, which is unusual for me—and somehow I made it back to Radišani."

"And now?" said my wife.

"Now nothing," I said, and stretched out on the couch. "We'll manage somehow until tomorrow."

"Tomorrow is tomorrow," said my wife. "If they said today after 3:00 p.m., then you'll go today after 3:00 p.m., and that's final!"

"I don't have the strength!" I said.

"Oh yes you do," she insisted, "besides which it would do you good to get out for a bit instead of lying here in front of me, despising everyone. Do you know what happened to me a few days ago?" She began to recount a story in which she apparently met a teller at the market who was selling onions and leeks on the side. Supposedly, she was doing it to earn a bit of extra cash because the money she earned at the bank wasn't enough to pay her children's university fees to study Law and Economics at the university in Skopje.

"Well, university tuition is expensive here!" I said irritably.

"Look, just go and get your card and stop lecturing me! And on the way, sort out that business for your granddaughter at the university," she said, and walked off in a huff, a sign that the conversation was over, and that I had to fulfill my obligations without further delay. I recalled the old saying, "Don't put off till tomorrow what you can do today," gathered my strength, and went to the university first.

"You'd like to register an enrollment for the semester?" said the friendly admin clerk, and smiled at me. "No problem!"

She disappeared somewhere, and when she returned said to me: "Our manager's not here to sign. Can you come back tomorrow? Here's a confirmation slip that we've retained your file!"

What else could I do, I ask you? That's what my Monday was like. That's how my week began, all topsy-turvy as they say. I took the slip of paper, popped it in my pocket, and walked to the bank downtown.

I stood in the line, and after a short while the teller appeared, completely unnerved.

"You're all here for a card, huh? What were you thinking, coming here now, at such an inappropriate time, creating a disturbance? Sign the slip and come back tomorrow! I can't do anything today! Can't you see that it's chaos out there? That there's a demonstration going on outside? I've been ordered to close! Sign the slip of paper, take it with you, and come back tomorrow!" and she literally shoved us outside.

I didn't know what to say. Outside it was getting dark. The days were short. It was the end of December. We were in the thick of winter. The man who came out with me from the bank looked a little dumbstruck. His mouth was half open as if he wanted to say something, but he was rendered speechless by the rude behavior of the teller, who could barely wait to get rid of us so she could go home and perhaps, as my wife said, moonlight as a garlic or onion or leek vendor, selling to her neighbors at night when no one would recognize her.

In all that kerfuffle, I suddenly remembered that in a nearby apartment building lived a close colleague of mine, an archivist. He was one of the rare true friends that remained in my life. We freely borrowed and lent things from one another. I wasn't too shy to just drop by and ask him for a loan of a few denars, enough to scrape through the week, because along the way I remembered that old saying, "If something goes wrong on Monday, your whole week will be topsy-turvy." And it was the third week in a row for me that my Monday was a total mess!

I rang the doorbell, and he opened at once. He smiled and appeared truly delighted to see me. But he also looked quite old. We'd all aged, only we didn't want to look in the mirror.

"Forgive me," I said, "but I need five hundred euros. I'll pay you back next Monday."

"Come in and warm up, and have a drink," he said.

"No, I don't want anything, and I no longer drink. The doctors say I've drunk my share!"

Without a word he gave me five hundred euros, and said to me: "No hurry, repay me when you can. It's a shame you won't come in and have something to drink. I have some excellent rakija," he said, "it would be top-notch heated up with some sugar!"

"Thank you. Thank you so much," I said, and as I was leaving,

I suddenly thought and said to him, "Do you want me to sign a slip of paper?"

He said nothing. He just blankly and with apparent ease registered this gratuitous, ironic remark, addressed to the wrong person. Fully understanding, he gently patted my shoulder while leading me down the hall to say goodbye. Feeling remorseful on account of my blunder, for a moment I felt as if I'd drunk that warmed-up rakija he'd offered me, and my soul grew warm. With tears in my eyes I made my way over to the No. 57 bus standing opposite that went to Radišani.

# JAGODA MIHAJLOVSKA-GEORGIEVA

## *Imrul from the Beach*

SOMEONE BEHIND HIM called out his name. He stopped. Even before he turned around, he knew who it was, what he would ask, and what his response would be. Yes, who else could it be if not the Coalman?

"How's work today?" the Coalman approached him.

He asked the same thing every day when they met. Followed, as always, by:

"Care for a smoke?"

"You know I don't smoke," Imrul droned impassively.

Then, with a bored look on his face, he began poking at the sand with one of his shoes; those shoes of his that were two sizes too big, that of a morning would slap loudly with every step and fill with small stones, and of an evening would become too tight because his feet swelled from all the heat and walking.

The Coalman—so called because of his coal-black skin—lit a cigarette, and spat a juicy gob in front of him:

"Bloody hell! I've only sold one transistor radio. The boss'll get mad again. Why doesn't he give me one of those display boards with wristwatches, or with those women's trinkets, and then see if I come back empty-handed. Not these portable radios with flashlights. Goddammit, who'd be crazy enough to light up the beach in broad daylight, huh? Have you ever met anyone like that, huh? As for the radios, they're another useless bit of rubbish. They blare out some music for a few minutes and then . . ."—he made a throat-slitting gesture—". . . they just croak. That's the best they can do." He contemptuously held up the small, garishly multicolored device to Imrul's face. "Nothing but Korean crap! Yesterday, one of these guys who bake in the sun in skimpy trunks almost smashed my head in with it. Can't blame him, though; it didn't take him long to work out what a piece of junk he'd bought."

Imrul had heard all this a thousand times before. He remained silent, while the pile of sand before his oversized shoes grew bigger and bigger.

"And you're even worse off than me." The Coalman took a last drag of his stinking cigarette. "Those needles and threads of yours, they're Chinese-made, aren't they? . . ." he wanted to tease Imrul, but started to cough. Without finishing his sentence, he just waved his hand and walked off, swinging the transistor radio that was blaring loud music.

For some reason Imrul felt like calling him back. For no particular reason. Not because he had anything to say to him. The Coalman wasn't a close friend, nor did he like him, but watching him stride away, he suddenly felt very much alone. The beach seemed longer and wider than usual, unusually empty despite the hubbub surrounding him. The sun was slowly beginning to set, but the place was still teeming with people sitting or lying stretched out under beach umbrellas, and swimmers, and children running around. Instead of calling out to him, Imrul stamped angrily with both feet on the pile of sand, and as he headed off shouted in a voice louder than usual:

"Hey there, folks! Buy a . . ."

As always, he couldn't remember the rest of the sentence that in its entirety went: "Buy a magical automatic needle-threader." He had rehearsed it repeatedly to himself when alone. But then as soon as he opened his mouth to bellow it out, feeling certain that he'd managed to memorize it, a sound would escape him, a half-formed word, whole words even, or they came out jumbled

. . . Ah, that terrible language, English. Here everyone will understand you in English, the boss had advised them. But, for Imrul, it was a language impossible to pronounce.

It wasn't the first time he lost heart and gave up. That's why they don't buy anything, he complained to himself. How can they buy something if they don't know what it is? He dragged his feet along the sand, staring blankly at the miniature gadget in his hand. His backpack was filled with them. He could count on the fingers of one hand the number of people who'd recently bought one. Those crazy Chinese, coming up with new things all the time . . . he turned his anger against them, refusing to level it at the boss, or even at himself, for ending up with these to sell, that day when the goods were being divided among the group. Others who were luckier or who'd spoken up had fared better. Some had gotten earrings, necklaces, and bracelets to sell, others scarves, while still others got bags, sun hats, beach umbrellas, wristwatches, sunglasses.

Maybe because he was the youngest, barely twenty, and because he was a newcomer and quite reserved, they had dumped Imrul with "the Chinese"—that's what he called the gadgets. At first he couldn't figure out what they were for and how the needle actually managed to be threaded automatically. Then the boss told him, it's precisely because they can do that that everyone will be amazed and willing to buy them. True enough, they were amazed, but they weren't buying. Who gives a damn about sewing and mending when they're on the beach—the Coalman had poked fun at him countless times—or these stupid portable musical flashlights I sell? Not to mention the difficulty of saying the wretched sentence properly, the tongue twister that it was.

He felt weighed down. Not because of his backpack—"the Chinese" were light—but, nonetheless, he took it off and sat down on the sand. If only he had someone he could share the burden with, that sudden heaviness that overcame him . . . The Coalman, he said to himself, if he had stayed, I would've had a smoke with him this time, even if I choked to death on it, regretting that he hadn't called out to the Coalman to come back, despite the fact that he wasn't a friend, or even someone whose company he enjoyed.

Truth is, Imrul couldn't say he had any friends even in his homeland, Bangladesh, and much less here, in this land, whose name he couldn't even get right. He had a few acquaintances among the group he arrived with earlier that summer, but none he felt close to, none he could tell that he wasn't feeling well, that at times he felt like puking his guts out in those long days and nights as the ship sailed and sailed with them crammed below deck . . . Many times he regretted ever having left at all, not knowing where exactly he was going, only that, somewhere over there, he would earn money and return rich. Just how rich, well, that was something no one told him, nor did he ask how, and with what kind of work. The boss, he'd explain everything to them as soon as they arrived. That's what they were told. And until then they should talk less, sit still, and not cause any trouble. That's exactly what they were told, almost threateningly, talk less, sit still, and don't cause any trouble!

Serves you right, you miserable wretch! he reproached himself bitterly. Look where your talking less and not causing any trouble has got you! And he kicked a stone that was poking out of the sand in front of him. Needles and thread! He kicked it far away, all the way to the water . . . And you sit here quietly, you miserable loser. Well then, just sit here and rot!

He recalled the girls from earlier that morning, twins by the looks of things, with long blond hair still wet after their first swim. Oh God, how they'd laughed at him when he showed them "the Chinese." "Needles and thread!" one of them sneered sarcastically. "Are you crazy, or do you take us for fools?" She twirled a finger at her temple, while the other girl showed him her lovely bum with the thong bikini pulled tight between her buttocks. "Shall I sew this up here—what do you reckon, huh?" she giggled shamelessly. Had the ground opened up and swallowed him then and there, it would not have saved him from the shame. His ears were still ringing with the nasty sound of their laughter as he rushed away from them. Humiliated. Almost fleeing.

Yet they said a few words to me, and that's something at least. He smoothed out the pile of sand he'd formed between his feet. As for the others . . . he formed a new pile, smoothed it out again . . . when I approach them, they just look right through me as if I don't exist, as if I'm invisible, not even a hello, nothing . . . He flattened the sand fiercely with both hands. Or they'll wave me off impatiently and turn their heads away. Am I a fly, or am I a human being? What am I, huh? You brush off flies like that, you morons! His heart clenched painfully . . . They don't have to buy anything, that's not what I'm talking about, but a simple "Thank you, I don't need it, goodbye," or at least just a smile at me . . . Pounding the sand with his fists, he inadvertently squashed a bumblebee that was scurrying away. That poor little thing, Imrul stared at it sadly, innocent of any wrongdoing. He lifted it gently with two fingers, and became even sadder when he realized its buzzing was growing fainter and its little legs were wriggling more slowly. Less talking and not causing any trouble, just like this! He let out a bitter sigh, recalling that pitiful "sitting still" below ship's deck.

He put the sample "Chinese," which he always carried in his hand ready to display it to anyone showing the slightest sign of interest, inside the backpack with all the others, pulled the straps tight, stood up, and slung it over his shoulder. Anyway, there's hardly anyone left on the beach. He looked to the west. I'll call it a day. The sun had just dropped into the sea, far away over there on the opposite side. He walked off mechanically, without thinking. It had been like that the whole summer long: at the end of the day his feet would grow weary and tired and, if not from sheer habit, they might have refused to take him back to the camp, to the others . . . to the boss. They're probably all back there by now and, once again, I'll be the last to arrive. Imrul grew alarmed and quickened his step.

Hurrying along, his mind blank, not seeing anything, he almost trod on a pile of sand raised between someone's bare feet, and even worse, almost stepped on those feet as well. He stopped at the last moment.

"Sorry," he said jumping back, "I didn't see you."

"No worries, mate," the boy with the bare feet smiled at him, quickly smoothing out the sand with both hands.

He was no older than sixteen. To Imrul he appeared somewhat uneasy, as if he'd been caught red-handed. The same as me and my pile of sand a few minutes ago, he said to himself in amazement, and made ready to move off.

"Hey, wait," the boy stopped him. "Are you in a hurry?"

"Not really, but . . ." he was surprised.

"What are you selling?" he raised his eyes and looked at him.

"Nothing. I'm not selling anything," he flicked his hand, noticing that the boy's eyes were red.

As if he's been crying, he thought to himself. But these brats on the beach don't cry, he thought again. They come here to enjoy themselves, not to cry! He must've had a long swim, that's what caused it, the salt. He studied him more closely. The boy was wearing Bermuda shorts, nice ones, and a well-known brand of sunglasses, not those cheap ones that Imrul's colleagues sold. They were propped up on his forehead, his hair tied up in a short pigtail. And his eyes, yes, they were red, bloodshot even.

"What's your name?" the boy pulled down his sunglasses, perhaps because Imrul was staring at his eyes.

Imrul reluctantly gave his name.

"So you're from Bangladesh too. You've come from afar, huh? There's a lot of you here this summer, more than last year." The boy remained sitting, while Imrul stood beside him. "Do you have a sea over there?" he smiled agreeably.

Imrul shook his head vaguely. What he wanted to say was, even if there is one I've never been to it . . . or, even if there is one, it's not where I live. He said nothing. He thought it appropriate now to ask the boy his name, something about his land, anything. Instead, he took the backpack off his shoulders, loosened the straps, and poked around inside it with both hands. "The Chinese" rustled in their tinfoil packaging. He didn't have time to wonder at himself and his own intention, that's how suddenly the idea came to him. But, yes, that's exactly what he did. He tipped out a whole handful of gadgets between the boy's feet, in the spot where just a short while ago there was a pile of sand, now smoothed out.

"What are these?" the boy asked with marked interest, as if it were a matter of the greatest importance to him. He asked in a way that no one before had asked. Ever.

"Magical automatic needle-threaders." Imrul got out the whole sentence in one breath. It was the first time he'd managed it, fluently, without a single mistake. And he began to laugh out loud.

The boy joined him. They laughed together.

"Here, take it," he handed him one, still laughing.

"I don't have any money on me. I didn't bring anything with me," he pointed around him. There was no beach towel, no sunscreen, nor even any kind of bag.

"Take them all." Imrul shoved a handful of "the Chinese" into the boy's hands, the tinfoil packaging glistening, as if a ray of sunlight had returned from behind the sea in the west. "They're yours."

The boy took them in his open palms.

"Thank you," he said simply, without asking him why he was giving them to him, without questioning what use needles and threads would be to him. As if it were all understood. "I didn't tell you my name." He stood up, extended his hand in greeting, and firmly squeezed Imrul's hand, saying his name. "I'll be here again tomorrow. So . . . come by . . . I-I-I mean . . .," he stretched out his words a bit, "if you're up for a drink . . . I'm on my own too . . .," he smiled as if to justify himself.

Imrul didn't hear him out. His ears were hammering. A lump stuck in his throat, and strangely, a joy like never before stirred within him. He grabbed the backpack and slung it over his shoulder in such a hurry that he didn't even tighten the straps. He took off without turning around, almost running.

"See you!" was the last thing he heard, not stopping until he disappeared far from the boy's sight.

Then he took off his shirt and shoes, and waded into the water in his pants. He didn't know how to swim, so he stayed in the shallows, just up to his knees. It was the first time he had touched the sea. And the first time he felt like crying his heart out. He splashed his face and wept. Again and again . . . until his eyes became so red they hurt. Until they became bloodshot.

# ALEKSANDAR PROKOPIEV

## *Fragmente Meiner Mutter*

*My mother's eyes are like*
*two ponds from a fairy tale . . .*
— A lullaby

*Algernon: All women become like their mothers. That is*
*their tragedy. No man does. That's his.*
— Oscar Wilde, *The Importance of Being Earnest*

THE HOUSE IS shared, but she has her own separate entrance, with dark-stained timber Venetians drawn across the stairs and along the small balcony. When she wants to summon me, she raps a few times on the wall that separates us. There is no direct door between us; rather, it's necessary to skirt through the yard to cross the distance from my entrance to hers. If she's angry, she shuts herself inside and doesn't respond to my calls through the wall. Then it's as if her section of the house—the western part—is a separate, independent, freestanding home, through whose windows, in the dim light from the television, her straight-backed, youthful silhouette can be seen pulsating. (Critics are forever pointing out the real/unreal dichotomy of my canvases: to them, the city is seemingly captured from an aerial perspective, with tiny puppet-like figures moving along the pavements, the streets empty of traffic, and with buxom—in the critics' words "astonishing"—female nudes out on balconies, screened behind loose shutters. As if to make plain what I so clearly see when my mother gets angry and doesn't want to speak to me. I lock myself in my part of the house, and at times, putting on a sweater, I turn off the lamps, climb up to the small window in the bathroom, and peer outside—what I see then, I paint later on.)

* * *

The armor comes apart, hanging open in the middle like an old tattered shirt that's missing several buttons. The sharp pain I felt as the Black Knight thrust his sword deep into my shoulders subsided, replaced by a tingling sensation like that from a small scratch. I transform imperceptibly from a White Knight—the tournament favorite reigning supreme—into a sniveling little boy, who, since becoming impaled on the fence outside in the yard, and now lying in an awkward bundle on the pavement with his barrel-shaped body, is crying, and also dreading his mommy's reproofs, because he's foolishly torn his flannel shirt. And in this new, undignified form, I come to the realization that the Black Knight—the negative reflection of my "white" self—without malice, amiably one might even say (as if his sword is one of the illustrations of the letter "S" in an elementary school primer), painfully, but also gently, wounds my heart, to both toy with and punish me at the same time.

If I sleep alone or with Viki, as soon as I wake up, I write down my dreams in the notebook that's always at hand (I've filled six of them so far). However, I don't paint the dreams, perhaps just a few details from them. What ends up on the canvas is that which is truly seen with my awakened eyes—and not my sleeping eyes. I keep the dreams safe in the notebooks as if they were secret treasure chests. Sometimes I read them to Viki, who then attempts to interpret them—a delightful, somewhat illicit game that, when we're in bed, arouses our willing, naked bodies.

When I spend the night with Miki, things are a bit more complicated. We've been together almost four and a half months. She knows nothing about the notebooks. If a dream occurs, I try hard not to forget it while Miki's in the house, that is, until a quarter to seven in the morning. As acting secretary of a company doing thriving business, she leaves the house, dressed and made up, no later than a quarter of an hour prior to the start of the workday. I kiss her behind her ear, to avoid smudging her makeup, and wave to her once more through the half-open door as she hurries off down the street, heels tapping on the pavement. I lock the door and immediately write down my dream in the notebook.

* * *

"What do you think—why exactly in the drawers?"

"I don't know. They were there."

"Had you hidden them?"

She's probing my subconscious again.

"They were adorable. Small, dwarfish, with thick yellowish-red fur, and white bellies."

"You often dream in color. Because you're a painter. But you never . . ."

"I know what you're going to say. 'You never transfer your dreams onto canvas. But both are part of you—dreaming and painting.'"

"They weren't ordinary. That's what I said to her: 'They're not ordinary mice. Don't throw them out.'"

"Perhaps even you wanted to be free of them. Drawers, mice—all of that is tied up with your subconscious."

"I don't know. But she threw them out in disgust."

"And you knew there were cats outside."

Now she's going to ask me about her.

"She's appearing to you again, isn't she?"

"I knew she'd find them."

"When you dream of her, your subconscious breaks through. From the lower regions."

"Just imagine it—she replied to me in Latin. When I tried to defend them. 'They're filthy mice,' she exclaimed, '*mus musculus*! *Mus musculus*!'"

"Really?"

She thinks it's funny.

"You're the one who remembers my words, I don't. But that bit in Latin . . . Maybe it wasn't really like that. Perhaps I just made it up."

"Wait, doesn't it sound to you like a diagnosis? Or like a formal censure?"

"I think that's exactly what a mouse is called in Latin." (And what will you say to me now?)

"I really like your lips when they're half open like this."

\* \* \*

Mother combined New Year and her birthday in a two-part celebration at her immaculately maintained residence. "Like a Catholic," she jested. "That's why I look younger every year."

The program was known in advance: on the first day, at noon, the bell typically announced the arrival of the flummoxed uncle, the subdued aunt, and the seemingly petrified cousins, whose protruding front teeth failed to inhibit their impishness. "Good day, Aunt. Happy Birthday and we wish you good health and happiness," they recited each year, scowling—the same greeting my mother awaited with a half-smile, with which she would endure the aunt and uncle's slobbery kisses and the cousins' bird-like chattering. The next hour, until the beginning of lunch, we parted ways: the children in my room, the adults in the living room. As soon as the door was shut, my cousins, acting in accordance with their front teeth, immediately revealed their predictable, rabbit-like dispositions. All at once, they'd clamber onto the bed, and with skirts raised shamelessly, jump all over it like wild beasts. After that, without any prior warning, their seemingly delicate bodies would leap toward the trunk in the corner—for a moment, the room would be transformed into a battlefield littered with mangled, broken toys. Strangest of all, they did all this silently, without the slightest hint of a sound. My furious reaction, which normally followed, was never regarded by the adults as an attempt on my part to subdue the little monsters;

rather, it was seen as a whim. And then, while fawning over my aunt in a vain attempt to calm her down, my mother would say icily: "You should be ashamed of yourself. They rarely come to visit us." As punishment, I was made to clean "the hunting ground," prompted by my mother's terse, bitter rebuke—"just look at all this mess, what's the matter with you!"—feeling miserable and misjudged, knowing full well the sly devils were laughing at me behind my back. However, there remained a chance for me to at least get back at them a bit—while they used their knife and fork in "proper" fashion, they ate greedily, shoveling down the white meat of the turkey slathered with mushroom sauce, but I imagined what they and my aunt had been served up instead was roast skunk in cockroach sauce. When in due course the Zserbo torte was served, or better still, the equally crumbly Kasato torte with chopped biscuits, small chocolates, jellies, and dates, my vengeful imagination worked overtime with rapture—they ripped into the food with their bad teeth, stuffing down dirt mixed with dog piss, finely chopped dried rats' tails, glass, crushed aspirin, mosquito eggs, bird shit . . .

* * *

The second evening was reserved for friends, three couples with whom my parents had been socializing since their student days: the Karajovskis, Šterjovskis, and Kiseličkis. An association strengthened by the rehashing of old stories and anecdotes from their shared time at the university in Zagreb (as greenhorns at the start of a new episode in their lives; or lying side by side on carelessly made, lumpy mattresses in the warm halcyon days; or packed rowdily together inside the Šar Mountain cable car, below which swayed the fir trees; or sitting in the yard of our recently set up prefabricated house, where the old custom of having a few acres of land outside of town still prevailed), always pumped up with laughter like colourful New Year balloons, and tied together inseparably in a witty, loquacious, and high-spirited circle until the husbands' deaths.

In accordance with the close relationship between all the parents, I considered their children, of indeterminable ages (the oldest, Ikica, now Dr Jovan Šterjovski, neurosurgeon, is three years older than me, the youngest, Inče, now Jasmina Kiselička, editor of the music program on RTV Macedonia, is six years younger than me), as members of my extended family, as numerous sociable relatives with shared games, secrets, and jokes. Later on, it was we children who, one by one, were the first to break the oath of allegiance, "One for all, and all for one." Puberty was much stronger than the Musketeers' oath, instilled in us that August night in the open-air cinema in Varna. But at that time, at Mother's birthday celebration, to me my parents' friends' children were like a soothing balm after the previous unsuccessful day with my cousins. The door between the living room and the playroom was left wide open to make way for the carefree enjoyment and unbridled innocence of human nature. The loathsome, unpleasant world of yesterday spent with the cousins, the aunt, the feces, and the dead rats was completely erased. I felt warm and safe ensconced among the tangle of playmates stretched out on the rug. Some of the adults—often my father—would flop down among us, relaxed and happy, and play a word association game, or cards, or marbles (with a colourful metal ashtray standing in for the "shallow hole"), after which he would boisterously return to the living room.

After my father's death, my mother discreetly broke off contact with that circle of friends, gathering around her instead her former classmates from high school, all of whom were retired widows. Their excessive attachment to one another was confirmed by the objectionable chatter that emanated day and night from her part of the house, making its way firstly through the thin wall, and later on, in those few moments as they were hopping into the Volkswagen, spreading over the yard like a sudden rush of rain, never failing to chase away the startled sparrows. Once all four of them had packed into the car, my mother—the inviolable one, firm and upright—occupied the driver's seat, and with a spirited start, changing immediately into second gear, drove off with her faithful, cramped colleagues toward the big, intimidating city.

* * *

*My dear son,*
*Ever since it turned cold, I've kept wondering whether you remem-*
*bered to look in the bottom of the closet (below the jackets hanging*
*in the garment bags). That's where your quilt is. I wanted to call*
*you, but your father was certain that you would have seen it after*
*opening the closet.*

*I hope that you haven't caught a cold. Take extra care because*
*these first few months at the Academy are vital to acquiring confi-*
*dence, and for the professors to get to know you. Go to classes regu-*
*larly. Learn to get up early in the morning, by 7:00 a.m., and after*
*a small bit of exercise, get dressed right away and eat something in*
*one of the pastry shops nearby. That could serve as taking your short*
*daily walk. But before you go out, don't forget to open your window*
*wide so that everything gets a good airing. After breakfast, go back*
*immediately (don't spend more than half an hour outside), clean*
*up your room, so that by 8:15 a.m. you'll be ready for the Academy,*
*or, if you don't have any classes, for serious and steady work until*
*noon. Painting, as you yourself have probably realized, is learned*
*with persistent effort. In the afternoon, if you have no commitments*
*at the Academy, you can, after lunch, rest until 5:00 p.m. And then*
*after that, go back to painting again—if you're in your room, draw*
*the curtains so that you aren't bothered by the street lights. At night,*
*don't go to bed any later than 11:00 p.m. I'm not insisting you follow*
*this schedule; rather, take it as the advice of someone wiser than you.*
*Discipline, I assure you, is far more important than talent.*

*Don't keep food in your room, and look after your own personal*
*hygiene—that's necessary if you want to feel well. In your next par-*
*cel, pack your old shoes together with your dirty underwear, and*
*send them to us.*

*We'll wire you some money on Tuesday, so you should receive it*
*on Wednesday. Make sure to be at home. Prepare a budget immedi-*
*ately—set aside how much you need for paint, canvases, and pocket*

*money. That way you'll be sure to have enough to last until the end of the month.*

*Are you attending the printmaking lectures? Don't be obstinate. Listen to that professor, who—like it or not—is esteemed as an excellent educator. There will be time to indulge your whims when your studies are over.*

*Write to us and don't forget to send us your newest drawings. Place them between cardboard and tape them up to keep them safe.*

*Love,*

*Mom and Dad*

\* \* \*

"In other words, you were in prison."

"Yes, but it was pretty comfortable. Like one of those beautiful prewar buildings they call mansions. With thick stone walls and high ceilings . . ."

". . . decorated with sumptuous chandeliers made of white marble, lined with gold leaf."

"And lights that mimic candles. Precisely like that."

"And the windows?"

"Long, narrow, double-paned. You're wondering whether they had bars on them? No, on the contrary, when I parted the light, transparent curtain, I saw that I was on the first floor, actually even lower down than that, on the slightly elevated ground floor of the building."

"And then you escaped. Don't take it literally. In a basic sense, the dream is symbolic, anti-mimetic. It doesn't reveal anything; rather, it exists only inside the intricate world of the psyche."

She's so sexy, naked, and enlightening.

"Do you find the way I'm talking to you funny, as if I'm in college?"

Viki, that is, Dr. Violeta Kostova PhD, is without doubt the most alluring member of the female teaching staff in the Faculty of Philosophy. Next to her, the others remind one irresistibly of doughnuts, and some of the more ambitious—of retired members of the Communist Youth League. Viki, whether she's on television or behind the lectern (for "behind" read "under" in the case of the numerous student-voyeurs), is impressively attractive, especially to strapping youths between the ages of nineteen and twenty-three. Imagine the dizzying rush of excitement that would surge through those aroused students if they heard Dr. Violeta say to them in the two most influential languages in the world, which she had skillfully mastered:

"Wait, wait the order. Kiss me, touch me, down there. Put your finger in my mouth . . . *J'ai rasé mes poiles, tu peux les sentir. Veux-tu faire l'amour comme une bête? Il faut pas être très doux, pas doux . . .*"

". . . and after that?"

"I beg your pardon?"

"You seem lost in thought. I was asking you about your dream. Tell me, what happened after you escaped? And rub my back. Gently."

"Well, I jumped onto the pavement, which immediately transformed into a barely visible path in a forest in the middle of nowhere. I felt like one of those fugitives in an adventure film, who, covered with scratches, out of breath, and soaked to the bone—a fine drizzle had begun to fall, common in these kinds of situations—hacks his way through the inaccessible jungle, clashing with the twisted branches of the monster-like trees, behind which he is convinced other monstrous creatures lie in wait."

"Now, my shoulders a bit. And after that?"

"I hid. Actually, I huddled under a huge bush."

"What for?"

"I knew that someone was chasing me. And that eventually he'd find me."

"Saliva's built up in my mouth. Do you want some? Come here, take some . . . And? And who found you?"

"A midget."

"What?"

"A dwarf from my neighborhood. A midget. Dapper in appearance, in a freshly ironed green uniform, and with a dazzling fire helmet on his head. We called him that because, being short, he was compact, stocky, and had no neck."

"Did he scare you?"

"Not in the least. In the dream, just as in reality, he was a kindhearted, humble little fellow. Somehow he managed to stammer out that he had a drawing, a gift for me."

"A gift? Keep your hand there. From who?"

"He wasn't able to tell me. Drawn on the paper was some sort of room, a living room, with an oval table covered with a white cloth. Actually, the round shape appeared to have been drawn by a child's hand with fluorescent markers that clumsily strayed over the darker, also crudely drawn lines. Arranged on the table, with the aim of making them look neat, were plates, forks, and spoons. Around the walls of the room were arranged a few chairs. In the big vase in the middle of the table was a bouquet of roses. I don't know where I got the idea that they must have cost a lot."

"That's important."

"You mean cryptic. Or perhaps incorrect."

"Why incorrect? Roses, as far as I'm aware, are more expensive in winter, and she was born in December, wasn't she?"

\* \* \*

The damage, a small scratch on the rear bumper of the Volkswagen, is noticed, and: "Did you have another accident?!"—an expected, and perhaps for that reason a murderous pronouncement. Both friends present at the time immediately back her up, baring horse teeth smiles (more than emphasized by well-crafted dentures). "You never take care. Do you know how much the repairs cost me?"—the same contemptuous glance, the same insinuating tone (she's sixty-six!): that's how easy it is for the "irresponsible one" to suffer and, naturally, to endure the reprimand, like a twelve-year-old caught in the act with moistened underwear (you'll be short of sperm and you won't be able to have children!). My reply, predictable, hurried, stammered, as if I'd been stuffed into a small glass jar, in which my words become cloudy from taking in only short gulps of air that's expelled through lips clamped together into a fish-like pout: "I'll pay . . . I'll fix it . . . why are you yelling at me?" "I never yell!" Thus, in the immaculately clean classroom at the boarding school, the remarkably restrained Mutter delivers her lesson on obedience to her fearful pupil.

\* \* \*

At her own insistence, I had dinner with Miki at Beneks, a restaurant crammed full of wood carvings, with prominent displays of logos from world-famous companies behind a massive bar, and a forlorn-looking stag's head mounted on the wall (fortunately, there were no paintings). Inside the restaurant, newly made businessmen called loudly to the waiters by name. Last summer, one of those clean-cut waiters with the fixed stare of a groomed poodle turned me away because I was unsuitably dressed. In all honesty, I'd come directly from the studio—in my dirty smock and sneakers—but, at five in the afternoon, the restaurant was empty, and I dropped in just for a coffee. Since then, the thought of ever going back to Beneks hasn't entered my mind. But Miki, dressed in a skin-tight leather mini, a shimmering, beige, off-the-shoulder blouse, a red lace bra, and thong panties (she has never looked better—unless when she's not wearing underpants, which is vastly superior), stressed out yet again, dabbing blue lipstick on her fleshy lips, like a used Barbie doll, and whined incessantly, "Will you take me to Beneks for dinner?" which, for all her petty efforts, bore fruit. Besides, Viki was in Budapest, at some sort of congress on Art Nouveau. And so, in the absence of the preferred one, and after Miki, in a show of thanks, licked my cheek, slow and wet, so that she wouldn't cover me in lipstick, we went to Beneks.

Greeting us with a sneer was the same slick waiter from last year (a bad omen), who, predictably, didn't recognize me; instead, with prompt and obsequious service, he enquired smoothly: "Aperitif?" "Martini Bianco for me," Miki ordered, over-enunciating, as if practicing the correct pronunciation.

Just as she was bringing the glass to her half-open lips, holding the thin stem between thumb and forefinger, a smug voice

broke our mutual silence, which (apart from when she was sex-
ually aroused) was a common feature of our relationship:

"Good evening, Miss Miki."

She looked up coquettishly, but politely decided to swallow
her drink before replying:

"Ah, Mr. Dončo, it's you! I haven't seen you in ages."

Mr. Dončo, a small, solid man, made even shorter in appearance by his oversized black suit, with a pager stuck on his pat-
ent leather belt (director of "Agromak," Miki introduced him,
revealing all the lavish whiteness of her teeth), was accompanied
by one of those men who frequent these kinds of places, with a
thick gold Turkish chain amid the vigorous tufts of hair proudly
protruding from his unbuttoned shirt.

To cut a long story short, the next half hour went something like this: after he doled out various compliments to Miki
about her clothes and hair, Mr. Dončo remarked that the day
before yesterday he'd bought a new Honda, upon which his
companion with the gold chain effusively began to inflate the
speed, size, comfort, and power of the respective model in relation to other non-Hondas; Mr. Dončo remarked that during
this unbearably hot summer he'd have to flee to somewhere far
away. His self-possessed spokesman made reference immediately
to the gaming houses and yachts anchored off the beaches at
Montevideo where there was a ninety-five percent chance they
could meet up with Savičević from Parissaintgermain: "Where—
in Uruguay?" I asked him with the utmost erudition. "Nope—in
France."

After that, everything happened quickly: to my ignorance of
geography, he responded with insults, to my insults, he grabbed
me and threw me down on the floor. Miki began to scream, and
Mr. Dončo, in an unchanged and calm voice, to placate her:

"Cab! Somebody call a cab, help this man!" I heard his
appeasing voice somewhere off in the distance, while secretly,
beneath the table, he gave me a final, most painful blow to the
head with the tip of his "dancing" shoes.

The next thing I remember was the familiar face of my

childhood friend, Dr. Jovan Šterjovski, in his office at the Neurosurgery Clinic. "You've had a fall," he said to me kind-heartedly, "everything's going to be okay." He sat down on the round stool, which sagged under the weight of his two hundred and twenty pounds, wrapped in a white coat. That formidable body swiveled the concealed seat a quarter turn to the left, then to the right, and came to a decisive halt in front of me: "We'll stitch you up so that no one will be able to tell," he slapped my arm. "Is your mother well?" As he stitched me up, hugging me with his outstretched, thickset legs in white pants, which, peeking out from his coat, looked as if they belonged to a fat dwarf, he moved his lips silently as he once did when shooting marbles.

When I got home, my mother was waiting for me in the studio.

* * *

"Where have you been all this time? Some hysterical woman called to tell me that you'd been beaten up. Look at you! Who are you gallivanting around with, frittering all your time away?"

Her entire body was rigid. Only her lips moved as she uttered carefully chosen words: "Do you know what people around town are saying about you? At times, you disgust me."

"Leave me alone, you can see that I'm wounded."

"Yes, wounded—wounded in the head. You can tell that also from your perverse notebooks."

"What notebooks?"

"You know quite well, all that sexual nonsense you hide away under the bed like a teenager."

"Who gave you permission to go through my things? When are you going to stop controlling my life! I never feel at home in this house! You're the one who's perverse! You're the one who's selling all the paintings that father loved so much and collected for years!"

"That's my business. They're my paintings. I'll sell whatever I want."

"And Pandilov's print? And Mazev's! How could you? If not for father's sake, then for mine—after all, I'm a painter!"

"The house was falling apart. If I hadn't gotten that money to whitewash it, it would have looked like a hovel by now. Besides which, I bought a washing machine to wash your dirty clothes."

"Did you ever stop to think how much those paintings were worth? And you're comparing them with a washing machine!"

"Well, do you think that, at the age of seventy, I enjoy doing your washing? You should be ashamed, you worthless, ungrateful little drunk!"

I couldn't restrain myself. I pushed her. I was amazed at how easily she tumbled to the floor.

* * *

"I had to wait at the border for a long time," Viki tells me, giving me a hug, although she looks like she's just come from a theatrical premiere or an exhibition opening. In the Volkswagen, in a good mood, and looking quite stunning, she recounts the details of her trip to Budapest without pausing for breath: about Erzsébet Bridge—the white one—that's regularly scrubbed clean with huge brushes and soapy water; and the one at Széchenyi, with stone lions at both ends, that leads toward the eponymous library in the old castle; about the ancient Gothic church of King Matthias with its soaring towers, unexpectedly decorated with purple, green, and pink ornaments. When we arrived at the house, she was enlightening me about IKEA, the Swedish furniture company, which has a building right opposite the last stop on the blue metro line. "All the buildings and the store motifs are decorated in a solid baby blue and yellow combination," she carried on effusively, stepping elegantly inside the house, "including the sign, the flag on the roof, the gate in the parking lot, and the sales staff's caps." She catches sight of the canvas, runs over to it (finishing her story about Budapest—"I tell you, the entire city smells of gas"), stands in front of it (I notice her new leather sandals with thick heels, whose flesh colour overlaps with her ankle), emotion thinning her voice as it normally does whenever she sees a recent painting—"Why, this one's excellent!" "Too many details," I make excuses, which is typical of me. "The figure in it has to be completed. The background, the crowded room—in truth, I could paint over them, leaving just two or three things: the small, round table with the bright-coloured tablecloth, on which there are two cups of unfinished tea, and perhaps a dictionary that's fallen apart, but what's most important is the figure in the foreground—the battered doll with the small, whitish loop through its nose."

"A new puzzle for the Derridadaists," she purses her lips mischievously, then randomly asks: "And is there a connection between this little loop and the ones on your forehead?" She's referring to the three stitches that I tried to hide under my hair. "I hit my head down in the basement," and without needing to, I brush aside the guilty lock of hair. "You really hurt yourself," she looks over the scar with concern (even though it's clear she noticed it at the bus station and the whole time, while she was happily telling me about all those buildings in Budapest, she was waiting for the right moment to ask the question). "What were you doing down in the basement?" "I wanted to bring the white cupboard back upstairs. You know, the one from my childhood," I attempt to speed up my words, "the one my mother took down there after the death of Vanya."

"Please stop, I beg you. I know that story already." "Why 'story?'" "Because it's impossible," she spoke firmly as if in warning, "that she lived that long. There'd be a remnant left behind from those two years—a photograph, a handkerchief, or at least her date of birth. In this way . . ." "They took everything after her death," I try to explain to her, "her expensive clothes, her shoes, her little bed, the dolls. And the chiffonier. But it was too big to throw out, so they left it in the basement. 'Place a comb and a key on the face of the mirror,'" I repeat my mother's phrase from my dream. "That's Mutter," I say to her, "distant and impervious during Saturn's Golden Age, distant and impervious," I repeat, "to the death of her husband, and to the death of her child." "We all have our own good and bad days," she calms me down, cupping my face in her hands, but her eyes peer searchingly, "only, some of us reveal them to others, while others hide them even from themselves. If we consider things from an astrological point of view," she says, "then she's entitled to a second Moon, and you will finally see her as timid and sentimental. But is that what you really want? Mutter transformed into a teary old woman. What would you dream of then?"

"And why is it necessary for you to flip the facts," she continues. "About Vanya. And the scar. That's also a tale." "What do you mean?" "Well, just that . . ." she lies down on the couch, crosses her legs and feet, which in the sandals from Budapest appear even more toned and tantalizing. "Sit down." "I don't want to," I snap back. Almost imperceptibly, with just a small spasm of her left arm, she reveals that she too is tense. But her voice remains calm: "As you wish. Come on, don't get angry," she touches my arm. "What a funny thumb you have. Fleshy, and veined to the tip," she gently separates it from the other fingers and kisses it softly several times, holding it between her lips. "Don't be naughty," she whispers, warming my thumb with her breath with every "shh." "Do you like your little Viki? Do you love your little Viki? Say yes . . . yes . . ."

* * *

It's June. In the yard, ripe cherries drop delicately to the ground, or else overripe, shrivel up soundlessly on the branches. In the neighbors' yard, motionless and white, the sheets and nappies (the fat neighbors had a baby, chubby and quite vocal) defy the gloom like benevolent spirits. The cherries, the sheets and nappies, the cat sleeping quietly by front the door, the hose carelessly thrown onto the middle of the wet patch of grass after the ritual watering (one time, the neighbor found two half-naked neighborhood louts spraying each other with the hose and, without getting angry, just took it from them and continued watering the grass)—all of these things compel me to imagine these dutiful, lumbering clods and their chubby little offspring as withered beings, hung out to dry with their heads hanging low, while the crazed cat waits for them to drop into its salivating jaw. In vivid detail, as I once did with my cousins, I picture them screaming and whimpering, and in slow motion, standing there with legs straddled, soiling themselves as fear consumes them, being torn apart and digested down the greedy throat of the animal.

It's been six days since my mother last came to my part of the house. She hasn't once rapped on my wall.

I broke up with Miki immediately. The next morning, I phoned her at what she proudly refers to as her "office," but before I could even get out my first sentence, in a shrill voice she said: "There's no need to apologize. I've coped without you before. The director of Agromak has transferred me. A fine man, who knows what is and what is not proper behavior. I thought that you were also someone with good manners, and not someone who takes me out and leaves me stranded in the middle of the restaurant, in front of all those people. I need a serious relationship, not just someone who calls me when it suits him. I've had enough of all these screw ups—" I hung up on her without waiting for her to finish, and it was a predictable end to our physical assignations.

Viki, however, squeezed the truth out of me about the incident. I told her that I was sitting with Jasmina Kiselička in one of the cafés at the entrance to the park when an interloper bore down on us and wantonly began flirting with her. I was forced to beat him up. "Then what's the scar from?" I told her that he hit me with an ashtray. Her expression took on its familiar, inquisitive gleam. Then, leaning forward, she asked: "And the girl, Jasmina Kiselička. Who is she?" "Her? A childhood friend, I'll introduce you to her . . ."

The hands of the wall clock, one of the rare old items left behind in my part of the house, limply overlapped. Five more minutes to eleven p.m. The neighbors' baby, as usual, is screaming like the devil, accompanied by the syrupy lullabies of its parents, which sound pleasing only to them. I lower the roller shutter. I shut the door behind me. I come face to face with the painting still crowded with unnecessary trifles, in which I can barely distinguish the neglected figure with the loop through its nose. It's all so hectic. And this mother of mine who is behaving just like a hot-headed teenager. It's true that at the end of their lives people revert to childishness. Their bodies and their minds are as unstable as that of a five-year-old. I need to calm down. To finally get rid of the painting. I'm going to paint over the whole thing. In orange. And this unformed creature staring at me. How can she hold out for so long? Perhaps I hurt her? She fell. And she was dragging herself along the floor, tearing out her hair and howling like a distressed animal. Why doesn't she knock? Why have you shut yourself in there as though in the basement? No one will ever hear you. Not even your girlfriends. They couldn't care less about you . . . No one! . . . Do you have a child? Do you have a past? . . . Mommy, Mommy . . . Gordana! Rap on the wall at least once! Call me . . .

# TOMISLAV OSMANLI

## *Strained*

TWILIGHT FELL OVER the city and the moon hung low in the summer sky, just like Bobo Tuntov's loose scrotum, which on sultry days such as these felt heavier than normal. It swung hot and pendulous, wiggling left and right, and bouncing up and down as the ambulance, with lights flashing and siren on, whirred through the heavy and erratic traffic. As they wound their way through the stream of vehicles, Bobo pulled off the thin sheet covering him on the stretcher. In just his boxer shorts, inside which his cannonballs and torpedo rocked, he revealed a bloated belly, strained as tight as a drum and as huge as the dome of a Turkish mosque. He gasped for breath, panting from the heat as the vehicle negotiated the curves and bends and shortcuts to the emergency center. A visibly robust paramedic with a nose piercing lifted the stretcher and, underestimating Tuntov's weight, was startled by the load of his live cargo. At the same time, Tuntov groaned loudly out of fear, and let out a short tight fart, after which he felt a bit better.

"What seems to be the trouble?" without even glancing at him the doctor on duty at the emergency center asked mechanically. He was studying intently his annual leave notification that he'd only just received, and which in no way fit in with the prepaid package-tour arrangement with the divorced Head of the

42

Resuscitation Department. Moreover, it didn't take into account his already straitened circumstances.

"I feel strained!" briefly and breathlessly the patient replied, whose belly had attained impressive dimensions.

"We're all strained," the young doctor said, and he continued poring over the notification. Even at the end of his scrutiny of the document, and his thoughts on how to prudently justify taking the romantic getaway with the buxom redheaded department head, he still may not have cast an eye over the patient had he not heard a stifled rumbling sound.

"I beg your pardon?" said the doctor.

"I didn't say anything," replied the unrecognized successful businessman and current party leader, Bobo Tuntov. "They're rumblings. I tell you, I'm strained."

"Mr. Tuntov, is that you?!" said the young doctor, delighted at the important patient who'd found his way to his dull round of duty, which was taken up with two traffic accidents, a gunshot wound inflicted on a father by his son, a pinky chopped off in a spat between neighbors, and two stab wounds (caused by a broken beer bottle and a switchblade knife) sustained in a drunken barroom brawl, all of which entailed the same old tedious injuries and the same old even more tedious stories.

The room filled with the new rumbling sounds coming from the politico-businessman's stomach, which to the young doctor sounded like an audible declaration of identity.

"Delighted to meet you. I'm Doctor Kikirezov," he reached out and shook the hand of the well-known figure with the distended belly. "What seems to be the trouble, Mr. Tuntov?"

"Well, how do I explain it to you . . . it's my butt."

"In what sense?" the doctor moved slightly aside, anticipating some sort of tasteless joke from the well-known businessman and party leader, who consistently managed to stay in office, regardless of who was in government.

"In the sense that something's obstructed my bowel and I can't pass wind, apart from these occasional, strenuous discharges that only bring some slight relief."

"Oh, I'm sorry to hear that . . . and what, has . . . umm . . . caused the blockage?"

"It's as if I've got a whole computer stuck inside there, including the internet."

"I understand. To start with, tell me what you ate today."

"What didn't I eat! Everything, Mr. Kikirezov, everything that was served up to me. First off it was the computer. There were so many messages, I felt like swallowing it whole—casing, screen, and all. That's what I ate first, and now, I tell you, I can feel it inside my sphincter. I was satiated to some extent, but as you can see, I have the capacity for consuming large amounts. For breakfast at party headquarters I was served the new set of official party statutes, which, I have to say, I barely managed to swallow. And after that, a declaration of public housing support for single mothers, which I signed under the eagle eye of the female petitioner. After that I crammed her down as well, a plump specimen of quality single mother. I scoffed her down, naked as the day she was born (to a non-single mother), with a luxuriant bush covering her pubis from which I'm still suffering the effects of heartburn . . ."

"Well, Mr. Tuntov, it's your spirit that's keeping you going."

"Spirit indeed, but my stomach's going to burst. Can't you take a look at what's going on inside there?"

*Gargantua*, engraving by Gustave Doré
for *Gargantua and Pantagruel* by François Rabelais

"Certainly, just as soon as I get the instrument. Nurse, the sigmoidoscope, please! And prepare the patient for examination."

"At once, Doctor Kikirezov!" the nurse replied with the courtesy of a flight attendant. Slender and slightly stooped, she had jet-black hair with a large white crown, a shrill voice, and tiny eyes, which, although outlined with eyeliner, were made smaller by lenses as thick as the bottom of jam jars.

The nurse deftly brought over the short endoscope and handed it to the doctor, after which she lifted the patient's feet and hoisted him up by his heels. In the meantime, Kikirezov donned a pair of rubber gloves, a surgical cap, and put a green mask over his nose and mouth. Thus equipped, he began the examination. The nurse, with the look of someone who'd been forgotten and overlooked for a long-overdue retirement, flashed him a charming smile and went off enthusiastically. Kikirezov inserted the sigmoidoscope. Suddenly, before him he saw a seventeen-inch computer screen on which there appeared a steady stream of messages, and now also the reflection of the lens of his instrument.

"Incredible," said a startled Kikirezov, "I've never encountered anything like this in my experience."

"What did I tell you?! Well, my dear doctor, you're a young man. Wait until you see what else is in store for you. I got worse over time, my digestion became impaired, and now these problems have begun to appear. You should see what I used to pack away and process. I had a gut that could handle anything and the stomach for greater things, but behold, everything has its time."

"Just a moment," Kikirezov straightened up in his chair, and glanced at Tuntov's bloated face, "you mean to say that this condition is also apparent in others?"

"Ahh!" said Tuntov, "when I was a young sales representative, around your age, I also didn't believe it when I saw with my own eyes what my supervisors were capable of eating. It all began with the extravagant business lunches. In those days one lived modestly and the lunches were an opportunity for a person to fill up on food. But when the times changed and we all became more prosperous, when I saw all the things that my supervisors consumed, my weak stomach would turn over. 'Go on,' they'd say to me, 'don't just stand there—drink up! eat up!' And so all the food on the table would disappear: huge plates filled with hors d'oeuvres, platters with catfish and carp, pans with veal head, pots with pork pâté, whole mountain lamb, and honest to God, a roasted sheep or two. After that, whole suckling pig à la mode, which they polished off head and all, with the apple still stuck in its snout, until I noticed that, in their startling adolescent appetite, they began swallowing the plates in which the food was served as well. Porcelain serving dishes, silver plated cutlery, brass trays . . . all disappeared."

*Gargantua,* lithograph by Honoré Daumier

"It's not possible!" said the young doctor.

"Of course it is! Then those who were the hungriest moved on to the companies . . ."

"I thought that was just a metaphor for the transition."

"A metaphor, huh? Well then—where are all the companies? Poof! They've disappeared. Just you wait, others will show up, with companies lodged in their colons . . . I forgot, I also may have consumed a small company. Well then, can you do anything about the computer? I think I can feel every message that's being received. They're all requests and appeals, the main reason for my bloating. They're blocking me up and making me feel strained."

"At once, right away, Mr. Tuntov," said the doctor and returned to the optical device with which he broke through the screen, reached the casing, and succeeded in turning off the computer. "Is that better?"

"Whew! Yes, a bit," replied Tuntov. "Did you shut it down?"

"Yes," said Kikirezov, and he began to poke deeper inside with the instrument. At first he heard some music. After that, hardly believing his eyes, he saw three revelers who were sitting at a table with appetizers and singing a song that echoed through the depths, from the colon all the way to the appendix.

"Right then, who are these people?" said the young doctor.

"Introduce yourself!" said Tuntov in a tired voice. Relieved of the initial pressure, he began to breathe deeply, and freed from the painful tension and insomnia, he let his lower jaw drop and began snoring loudly.

"Look," said one of the revelers drunkenly, "the boss's swallowed a submarine! Here's the periscope."

"This is a medical examination, not nautical diving," replied Kikirezov with principled severity. "What are you doing here?"

"What do you mean what are *we* doing here—*we* work here," said the second reveler.

"And live here," said the third.

"We live life," added the first reveler, and then he started belting out a traditional folk song that echoed throughout the insides of the blissfully sleeping Bobo Tuntov. "*It's erupted! Šar Mountain has erupted . . .*" the song spread throughout the intestines of the great politico-business leader.

"What do you mean you live here?"

"Just that. We're political activists. We promptly got up Mr Tuntov's backside and we're not sorry."

"Get out of there, you great dopes! My patient will die because of you. He'll burst like a balloon!"

"Are you drunk or something, dude?" the singer-poet abruptly stopped singing, and turned on him. "Do you know how many others there are a bit farther along up here? We're first-generation colonists. Founding members. Wait till you see how many new members have gathered here. The difference being that they arrived here downstream. Tuntov gulped them down voluntarily."

"Is that why you founding members have blocked the exit?"

"Well, not for that reason. We're experts at seeking solutions. But now we're looking for them here. We've done enough work, let the newer members make an effort. Let them find a way out. Anyway, we're almost at retirement. Well then, dude, on your way. You're obviously not from this planet. You have no connection to reality. Off you go then. There are still many things here for you to see."

The probe is too short, Doctor Kikirezov thought to himself, and at that moment, a familiar voice startled him:

"Congratulations, Doctor! You've eased the patient's pain. He's sleeping like an angel." It was the nurse with the shrill voice, whose screeching covered up Tuntov's even snoring.

"Give me a longer probe!" ordered Kikirezov.

"Doctor, it's as if you're conducting scientific research," said the frustrated flight attendant.

"Yes, I'm taking a tour through this person's posterior. But nurse, did the Head of the Resuscitation Department call?"

"Doctor Svetla Cockova?" the nurse asked inquisitively, flashing him a conspiratorial smile as it suddenly dawned on her just how thorough the medical training was that he received. "No," she shot back curtly, "she still hasn't called!"

Kikirezov ignored her indiscreet reaction. He thought for a moment about his summer vacation with Svetla, her round buttocks, and the coppery bush concealed among her full thighs that got him all excited whenever he saw her, and drove him wild when he ran his hand over her Bermuda Triangle. It's going to be an adventure to remember, if I can just sort out the issue of those damned leave days that I'm short of, thought the young doctor, Kikirezov, who that summer planned to fully qualify as a specialist, and the following year work in the Resuscitation Department with Associate Professor, Dr. Svetla Cockova (until just recently Hadžiconeva). He would have remained like that, absorbed in thought beside the yawning rectum of his important patient, had he not been startled by a loud emission of wind that issued from it, forcing him, once again, to promptly don his surgical mask and give himself over to his inspection. This time he inserted the new, longer probe for a deeper examination of the bowels of the sleeping businessman and notable political tribune . . . He passed by the three drunken revelers, who in the meantime had moved on to a new song and who pretended not to notice him. Behind the first red bend, he discovered a conference room in which a team of party activists was running back and forth, dictating and tapping information into PCs and laptops, drawing diagrams and strategies on whiteboards on which posters with Bobo Tuntov's face were stuck.

"So, these are the activists then!" The young doctor could not get over his surprise at the sight of the crowds that thronged the insides—all the way to the colon—of the well-known public figure, who was currently lying on his surgical table in the emergency center, sleeping the sleep of first relief, but who by all rights, after what he had witnessed, should have been wide awake.

"Wow, what an organism," was the only explanation given by the inexperienced Kikirezov for the medical problem with which he had been shockingly confronted.

"Watch out, a camera's filming!" began shouting one of the female activists with the voice and appearance of Olive from *Popeye*, pointing to Kikirezov's optical device.

"Who gave you permission to enter here?" Some politico—a J. Wellington Wimpy lookalike—piped up before his apparatus.

"Bobo Tuntov himself!" said Kikirezov fearlessly and without hesitation. "Who else would let me in here?"

"Mrs. Tuntov, naturally," the ruddy-faced Wimpy said confused, and added: "She sometimes drops by here too."

"Here?" said Kikirezov, overcome with disgust at the thought of where their marital encounters took place. "Oh, it's clear to me why you're here, but as for Mrs. Tuntov coming down here, that really surprises me. She's a family woman . . ."

". . . And a member of the Executive Bureau of our party!" the ruddy-faced interlocutor made clear, and added: "Now please go away. In any case, you've seen more than you should have!"

"With pleasure," replied Kikirezov, and deftly turned the apparatus toward the next bend in the internal space. When, all of a sudden, he saw—a company. A neat little building consisting of two floors with a central entrance, and a neon sign on which, in attractive Cyrillic letters, was written "Tunbo Company." In front of the company—a rabble, a disorderly crowd.

Eduard Wiiralt, gravura

"How did you fit so many in here?" Doctor Kikirezov was astounded at the sheer number of inhabitants placed inside Tuntov's bowel, but he assured himself that, from now on, nothing further would take him by surprise, even were he to find here the Burj Khalifa and the Palm Islands in Dubai, where he had paid for his holiday with the delightful Dr. Svetla Cockova. He didn't ask a thing, because the table full of people was brawling and yelling and protesting, carrying banners to which Kikirezov steered the lens of his optical camera and read: "Give us back our company, which you ate for free"; "This was a bowel company, now we've become a company inside a bowel"; and even "Tuntov-Thief," and "Cord Workers Resort Ltd.," only he wasn't quite sure what the resort was doing there, and despite his recent promise not to be further surprised, how it was still possible for there to be gathered near the four-story workers' resort in Bobo Tuntov's stomach an entire miniature Lake Baikal.

*Capricho* by Giovanni Paolo Panini: Roman ruins and sculpture,1758

The young doctor's head was in a spin. He raised his head from the apparatus, pulled off the mask, and began breathing loudly from all the excitement, when, like a delayed reaction, something flashed into his mind's eye. He quickly stuck his eye back on the instrument, aiming it directly at the beachfront resort. And there, spread out on a towel with a Hawaiian motif, he saw the naked body of a curvaceous beauty, lying on her front on a white plastic sun lounger.

At that moment, the beautiful woman turned around and Kikirezov noticed her voluptuous breasts and the luxuriant bush covering her pubis, bringing to mind the description that a short while ago his patient had given him. The single mother from breakfast, he said to himself. He began zooming in on the figure of the curvaceous single mother, who took off her sunglasses and placed them on the top of her red mane. Kikirezov was stunned at the sight. It was his beloved and the appointer of his medical career, Dr. Svetla Cockova herself. Sensing she was being observed, the curvaceous beauty began posing with smiles and crossing her legs, which gave her gleaming coppery bush a special appearance with alternating patterns.

"What are you doing here?!" shouted an agitated Kikirezov straight into Tuntov's partially unblocked opening, because the naked beauty was none other than his love's hope and destiny, the mature divorcée and Head of the Resuscitation Department, who instead of being at work, was lounging around in a suspect belly with all sorts of different people.

"Pussy cat, is that you?" she replied crossly.

"It's me, who else! And what, may I ask, are you doing stuck inside this great oaf's duodenum?"

"Which oaf?" Bobo Tuntov awoke from his deep sleep. "Doctor, I need to go!"

"Keep quiet, you swine. What haven't you shoved inside yourself? Well, even my personal and professional future!"

"What have I got to do with your future, young man?"

"Everything, everything! You ate my future for breakfast, that's what you've done. You've been eating my future since this morning, and I had no idea until just now that that was happening to me!"

"Doctor, it's getting serious!" Tuntov, the political tribune, called out in panic, pointing to his strained stomach that began to shake, as if inside him an underwater earthquake had occurred.

Kikirezov took no notice of him, and returned to his communication with the head of department.

"I'm having a bit of a rest, sweetheart. Well, perhaps even I have earned the right to a bit of relaxation!" she replied gently to him from inside.

"We were meant to go on holiday together, and to a beach— not a lake, and especially not one inside the cavity of this turd!"

"Kikirezov, watch what you're saying!" Tuntov called out loudly.

"Get dressed at once and come back here!" shouted Kikirezov into the businessman-party leader's rectum, but he felt his words weren't penetrating deep enough, and that they were being drowned out by a gurgling sound. He looked into the optical probe and out of the corner of his eye, coming from inside, he saw a murky tsunami, on which, together with the plastic sun lounger and the sunglasses on her head, was riding his doctor, fast approaching.

"Doctor, look *out* . . . !" Tuntov shouted a warning and couldn't hold out any longer before the more powerful decompression taking place.

Kikirezov just managed to pull the apparatus aside from the violently overworked bowel, when the nurse with the thick lenses and broad smile reentered the consulting room, opening her mouth to utter a kind, compassionate word, right at the moment when the first tsunami wave arrived from the stomach of the politico-businessman and entrepreneur, Bobo Tuntov.

Kikirezov ran out of the consulting room as fast as his athletic feet would let him, leaving the door behind him open. He stopped out front of the emergency center, and watched as Tuntov's tsunami poured out, flooding through the double doors of the entrance, flowing out the windows, inundating the clinic, spitting out companies, buildings, landscapes, banners, serving dishes, doors and windows, party activists, the redundant nurse, and the Head of the Resuscitation Department (who was borne along with it), carrying them somewhere far away from the clinic.

Doctor Kikirezov was terrified as never before: Well, he said to himself, and what if I and all of this are no more than one part of a far greater strain and pathological state of indigestion in a much bigger bowel?

# BLAŽE MINEVSKI

## *Dirt*

MY BROTHER REALLY liked to eat dirt, and I had to keep an eye on him to make sure he didn't do it. "Don't let him out of your sight. He's quick," my mother says, before heading off to the village tap to fetch water. And the moment she sets out along the path, the little fellow is already roaming up and down the yard, looking for ways to deceive me. Somehow, he always manages to sneak a mouthful of black dirt from over by the gate or some red dirt around the dried-up acacia tree or some white dirt near the cart pulled by Grandpa Ango's horse, which died standing up the first time he and Grandma Akta and their children set foot in the yard. Grandpa would sometimes sit on the cart with his head raised high, hold an embroidered handkerchief over his eyes, breathe in several times through his nose, and then loudly exhale through his mouth, asking me if I could smell the sea from behind the mountain. Naturally, my friend, I smelled nothing, but I didn't say a word.

When they were burying Grandpa, they threw dirt into his grave, but the hole refused to fill up. They even fetched some of the clay the fresco painters had dug up to paint the frescoes in the cupolas, but the grave still gaped. It wasn't until sunset that Father Bogomil noticed that Grandpa's mouth was open, as if he were exhaling. The priest ordered them to cover Grandpa's face with the handkerchief embroidered with the picture of the sea. Then he crumbled a bit of dirt between his fingers, splashed some wine over the mound that rose before us in the blink of an eye, and with his work done, he took his money and went off.

Only, most likely that's another story. I'll tell it to you when you're painting from memory, my friend. Now, in less than two hours the plaster will dry, and you won't be able to work on it any further; mistakes will be beyond repair. The wind quickly dries this paint made of clay soaked in quince tea; I can tell by the smell. In two hours, you must paint a definitive portrait of me, because you won't be able to fix it up later. The same way I can't fix what happened to my brother. I always tracked him down by his scent; he smelled like freshly dug earth. Only, just so you know, he was clever, and he never attempted to eat any of the dirt under the two winter apples, or any of the dirt by our abandoned loom, the wooden plow, the old broken barrel, or Grandma Akta's shabby bridal trunk. He'd sit on the cart, covering his mouth with the back of his hand. He's tricked me again, I said to myself. I'll catch him out, I thought. He won't get away with it. And so, one morning, while he was still sleeping, I tried to work out how he could tell which dirt to eat. Apart from the area by the acacia and the cart, he also relished the corner near the upper gate, next to the fence. I picked up a handful of dirt and sifted it between my fingers. It was soft and warm. It smelled like chamomile even though it was almost fall. The dirt around the acacia was like the watermelon preserve that Mom served to guests only at Dad's name day, when Dad was Dad, when he was still alive. Now he's dead and he doesn't have a name. Names are needed only by the living, I said to myself. Between the gate and the acacia lay the cart or, strictly speaking, the iron frame of the cart, brought to the yard sixty years earlier. I sat down on it, and tried to press my hand into the soil beneath it. My fingers sank into it like a knife through butter. It smelled like summer rain, like the first snowflakes that fell in the yard, like the herbs under the eaves that Mom pulled out by hand; it smelled like Dad when he came back from abroad, like our over-ripe fig tree, like the drooping leaves of the grapevine. It smelled like Grandma Akta's tears, even though I barely remember her;

memory is only part of what had once been true, so perhaps it's not her I remember at all, but just the mental image of her that's left behind. But, of course, my friend, you understand my meaning quite well. Paramount in what you're painting on the wall is you who remembers what he sees, and not I who sit on this stool, though you may look over at me to compare what you see with the memory that you're painting. And your scrutiny is also a memory of your scrutiny. I must tell you, sitting down on the cart I suddenly remembered that Grandma knew all the places around the village where there were different types of soil that were useful to her for various things. She knew where there was soil for sowing fruits and vegetables to make jams and pumpkin preserve with grape juice and sesame. She knew which clay was suitable for whitewashing the barn and the porch, which was for the floor, and which was for the fresco painters who were painting the walls of the church. This very church, this vestibule, to the right of the entrance to the belfry, here where I am still sitting and you are still standing. Me as a painting that's drying with the plaster, you as the red signature below it. I was sitting on the cart in the yard, and who knows where the memories that galloped through my mind were leading me. I heard the sound of waves in my ears. Then, as if I'd returned home from somewhere, I saw my brother sitting beside the acacia. He got up and set to work. The acacia was dried up, but tied to a big branch high up facing the yard was a swing on which we used to ride. The chains creaked. The swing was moving back and forth, and with it the acacia, as if it were playing a game. Now the little fellow was leaning back against the trunk, his hands scraping between his legs, digging frenziedly as if he were searching for the root. He soon raised a mound of dirt before him, scooping it upward and piling it against his belly. He went on digging, raising the dirt above his belly, piling it up to his chest. All the while he kept muttering to himself. I think he was crying. I heard him sniffling. He's just pretending to cry, I said to myself. I sprang off the cart. I wanted to go over and slap him. But just then, from somewhere deep inside the trunk, something stirred. A muffled creak emerged, and the trunk slowly bent backward. Just as I grabbed hold of the little fellow to lift him up, the acacia crashed to the ground, rolling down the hill.

The next morning, the birds that were used to perching on the tree flapped their wings in confusion, thinking back to the day before, wanting to land on the branch that they believed should still have been there. A magpie persistently swished its tail, thinking it was standing on the branch. And our cat almost climbed up to the place where we used to tie up the swing. It sprang into the air and did a somersault, then landed heavily somewhere in the nettles. Father Bogomil's dog was also infatuated with the acacia. He used to lean on the trunk with his front paws. Then he'd remember that he was a dog, he'd dig at the root protruding from the dirt, and cheerfully go off, together with the flies that followed him around, tracing another dog in the air. And now he did the same thing, only this time he smacked his muzzle in the dust, timidly looked up, curled his tail, and ran off whimpering as though in distress. For days I watched all the birds and animals that continued to believe the acacia was still there. I wondered how long it would be before they realized that it no longer existed, to forget it, even though I knew that memory is an eternal longing for the time we've lost. Only time that's remembered belongs to us. However, the memory of the acacia is not the acacia, I wanted to tell the birds that were fluttering in the air after they tried to land on the branch they remembered. Only a dove with a red collar behaved as though nothing had happened to the tree. It circled the yard, flew up over the house, and from there, flapping its wings in preparation to land, perched right on its old branch. Swishing its tail, it raised its head and began to coo, rejoicing. Naturally, I had no idea how it did that, but I knew that God must have created something much bigger than what can be seen, so some things will never be known. Down below the hill, Father Bogomil was measuring the trunk of the acacia. He measured it inch by inch, hooked a leg over it, and sat down. A short man sporting a mustache that looked like it had been stamped under his nose stopped along the path and asked the priest how long one needed to fast in order for his sins to be forgiven: "You'll fast until you return to the dust from which you came, because you are dust, and to dust you shall return," muttered the priest. The little man ran off as though he'd been scolded, disappearing like a mouse behind the pumpkins. The next moment, when I turned around to look behind me, the miracle that I'm now simply trying to recount had already occurred. What I'm trying to say is that, just as the dove never forgot the acacia, after you sign your name beneath the painting, I too will never forget what happened back then: a gaping abyss opened up before my strange brother and me. He was standing somewhere near the gate. I was on the other side where the acacia had once stood. A drizzle of light fell between us. Sprouting around the edge of the abyss, I saw red clover, thyme, and a shadow that rustled like an acacia. Chicks with silver feathers were scratching in the shadow. Their heads were similar to those of people. My brother was wearing his white shirt, but now it hung below his knees like a dress. He was still holding the back of his hand against his mouth and his head was crowned with a green wreath. Down below, at the bottom of the abyss, was Grandpa's cart, the loom that Mom kept need-lessly, the wooden bed we placed beneath the winter apple in summer, the table and chairs from beneath the vine, the pitchers that stood on the loom, the winch and the bucket, together with the well, Grandma's spindle and her old bridal trunk, and many other things. On different sides of the abyss were just the house, my brother, and me. When had he managed to eat that much dirt? I asked myself, leaning against the acacia that no longer existed. What will I tell Mom when she comes back from the fountain? I wondered.

And I don't know what I told her, my friend.

All I know is that my brother remained forever on the other side, alone with his memories. He never appeared again. He never came back, not even as a scent, or a swallow, although for years I watched our swallows bring grains of dirt beneath the eaves. Sometimes I still think that perhaps the dirt they're bringing from some other place is our dirt. Perhaps it smells like the sea, except I just don't feel that's true. Perhaps the tiny specks of mud that fall from the sky and get stuck under the eaves are part of my brother's dirt. My little brother who liked to eat dirt, and who I had to keep an eye on to make sure he didn't do it.

That's all, my friend.

Now I'll keep quiet so that you don't paint me with an open mouth. There's no time to correct mistakes.

# OLIVERA ЌORVEZIROSKA

## *The Irreplaceable*

JUST BECAUSE IT seems to me that it was much better before doesn't mean that it really was—perhaps later on, in the course of time, some things, which then just seemed like ordinary, average, everyday occurrences, were transformed into something beautiful, sturdy threads stringing together a necklace of petty trifles, fastened with a jagged clasp of the appalling, monstrous priorities of trivial sensations that are now best forgotten, but which at the time seemed so big—huge pendants—yet in hindsight seem so small—insignificant charms, so big as opposed to so small . . . it *was* now seems only to mean it *reportedly was*, not how it really was; bearing witness came later, in the future, the future apparently bore witness to the past (does that mean then that the past simply reported what might have been witnessed?); is there truth in grammar or does it act arbitrarily, treating events sometimes as *definitely*, sometimes as *maybe definitely*, and sometimes as *possibly definitely*, at other times as *impossibly certain—possibly uncertain* . . . or, then again, that which was and truly has been, or that which probably has been—did it make such a huge impression on us that it just seems real to us? Not now, at some other time, then, meaning *it's not real*, but more precisely—*it was real*; is it more or less the same as if I were to now start to call my dead mother on the number that I will always and forever know by heart, and as if she were able to lift the receiver—would that fact erase her death for a moment, or would her voice just emanate from wherever it has gone, remain for a while in the receiver, and then vanish into the impossible, although I'm not sure whether the impossible knows all the possibilities of a verb, does the category "reportedness" mean anything to it, or is everything that is impossible simultaneously witnessed . . . by whom? Who can witness what has never been— is it the same one who reports that which really was? Well, we ourselves say *apparently was* while we think *really was*, however, we need a much greater distance from what once was and is no more in order to keep the pain at bay; instead of *definitely was*, we say *apparently was*, as if so much time has gone by that we're unsure whether the thing has really sped through our life as a reality. Then again, with so many possible verb forms, what is reality? Everything that now exists will one day contend with the complex system of grammatical structures for the past; however, everything that we've hoped for and looked forward to at some future time, that we've counted on, appears to us now—and now is the future of an earlier moment—as nonexistence, absence, lack, we've lost that which we've been expecting before it arrived, it has vanished instantly, jumping from the future to the past tense, in flight over the present on wings of folly. The things that were irreplaceable become things that we apparently have never had, that we definitely never had, and the very fact of the cessation of anticipation hurls them into the past, which we yearn for, and to which we give all sorts of names, only not "reality," because reality has only one time, the time when the thing happens or doesn't happen—reality is as much *yes* as it is *no*, but it is never *perhaps, both/and, either/or* . . . The slipperiness of *yes* and *no* in relation to today and yesterday is the same as that of the truth and falsehood of everything to which we cannot attest with certainty, hence the standard use of *apparently was* before *definitely was*, even when talking about those things from which we will never recover; we say, *apparently it's hard to lose your mother*, meaning, *it really was hard to lose your mother*, or more precisely, *it is hard to lose your mother*, because *was* is insufficiently ripe for loss, which endures forever, and will remain in the present. There you see, once again, the future tense to emphasize the enduring present understood as some kind of eternity. Actually, for eternity there needs to be something new, a special tense, because neither the present nor the future are adequate for it, it wants both, plus something else. What else? Well, something else . . . and more than one thing, much more—many things, a countless number of them . . . eternity is just a false singular, because coursing through its veins is a substantial plurality, but . . . at the same time it's a countable noun, the mask of a regular singular over the true face of *singularia tantum*. Language needs to be restrained from head to toe, because one can never be sure whether it might escape us (or assail us): it escapes/assails us from all sides, it must be harnessed at both ends until we find it of use, until we want it to serve us and us to serve it, entrusting it with our personal stories as if to a faithful guardian, heaven forbid, as if to a distrustful guard. Great truths cannot be constructed; similarly, grown children cannot be raised in retrospect, so if we miss out on the right moment, be it for whatever reason, the sense of belatedness begins to weigh more heavily, it becomes a burden, a tax liability, interest that has to be paid and paid . . . so that they don't force you to withdraw into yourself? Who? Those dearest to you, without any malice on their part, force you to withdraw into yourself. Great truths cannot be constructed in the verb system created for minor things; it's not just the historical present that knows this, but also rather all of us together, speakers of the same language, beholders of the same nuances of time, feeling, thought. Great truths cannot be constructed at the front desk of memory, they scramble to get things "done," because they have links with the officials in life, in the shortest possible time they reach the head of the line, leaving behind them all of the things that up to then, only a fraction of a moment ago, had been submitted with their identity papers at the counter. A beep sounds on the cell phone with which you go to bed and wake up, waiting not for someone to call you, but just for someone to message you (what's contained in the text announced by the beep is already known, what isn't known is just the moment it was sent). Imagine that feeling of fighting against sleep as a battle with a terrifying beast to which you would immediately surrender and, despite your dread, imagine your own blood splattering everywhere as the beast is quartering you, and yet you desire it infinitely, to have it happen to you no matter what, as long as the phone squeezed in your left hand remains firmly silent, for the silence to go on forever, for it to never make another sound. Imagine the devastating blow of an ordinary call announcing a death, in contrast to the countless calls from others who tell you, or maybe don't, about the most insignificant things, often even just their gripes, imagine somebody asking for someone called Maya at your number while you're just waiting around for it to ring to find out that your mother has passed away. It would be awful for anyone were that mistaken Maya to interpose herself between life and death, because whoever it is who calls, while not the one you're expecting, doesn't presuppose that with the first disruption of silence you end up without a mother, who, in fact, you still have, be it in whatever form; you just wrongly assume that from that moment on you are without her. And what could that wretched moment change? Then again, loss can put an end to the anticipation, which is as heavy as a mountain, but it can also burden you with even greater anticipation, as heavy as two mountains— if you're the *mistaken Maya*. Those such as me who've never been the *mistaken Maya*, and who've been rung up by the very person they were expecting to call, know that what would make them happiest at that moment would be for it to be just a mistake, even if one mountain were to become two, nevertheless, nevertheless, the postponement of fearful anticipation is a way of taking cover from the end with the characteristic appearance of a July morning, a pallid sun, a Friday, the one following that dreadful one or the most dreadful Friday. Which of them is, actually, the most dreadful—the one in which things exist vitally or the one in which they formally end? Having a mother is a permanent condition, it's simply a question of having her in different forms: you have a living mother, you have a sick mother, you have a barely living mother, one foot in the grave with the toll of a single bell and, in the end, you have your mother in the form of death, which is final, permanent and incomprehensible, eternal. And then, after that the irreplaceable changes you with terrible speed, you start doing things you've never done before, if you've been sleeping on a low pillow, you start sleeping on two high ones, if you've enjoyed Russian classics, you exclusively read other types of books, if you've been writing prose abiding by all the orthographical and typographical rules, all at once you invest in *scriptura continua*, stream of consciousness precludes you from the need for plot, you experience physical pain in telling and in not telling, to which you submit, if not on a miserable scrap of paper, then on the miserable keyboard, the miserable monitor, always dusty, the miserable desk, the miserable spotted kitchen bench, white marble from the Prilep region, the miserable pots, including the medium-sized one with the broken handle . . . the miserable thought that it will never be the same again, as it actually was . . . The warmth of your childhood will never be sufficient to thaw your pain, you will slowly melt away without even realizing that that's it, you will slowly dissolve, continuing on to where you've been heading, to where you were headed, you will slowly fade away, and after who knows how long, you will be at the farthest point from your own birth, which we usually refer to as death. A projecting balcony, with decades-old unpainted bannisters, a view of the hospital grounds slightly obscured by garages—not even the view is the same anymore, because the hospital grounds are no longer "hospital grounds," from whose characteristics throughout your entire childhood and youth you determined the seasons outside and within you; rather, they're "the grounds surrounding Mom's death." For so many years you've been on the same side of the hospital wall, and now here you are on the opposite side: Mom's death—inside, and me— outside, a huge wall between us that can be leaped over in an instant, but that cannot be surmounted, because it's a concrete wall, because it's wrought with iron spikes, because it's stained with the blood of your brother's hand, because it's a wall between life and death. The hospital in which your mother gave birth, in which you and your brother, me and my brother, were born, the "hospital grounds" within which you grew up, within which my brother and I grew up, where my mother was operated on, where every Thursday for more than twenty years she gave blood at the Department of Transfusiology, where, from time to time, I collected her results, also on Thursdays after 1:00 p.m., and while walking through the tall grass I would read the sheet of paper— stating whether or not and how many tablets were necessary for her to take weekly—since that time I've despised percentages, because my fear grew out of them as a direct result of how much longer I would have my mom in living form . . . The hospital grounds through which we walked as a shortcut to the center of town, to the high school, to the mosque, to the old supermarket, became the longest and most difficult path. To take flight from the plot, that's what must be done at once, here she is, tugging at me with all her might, and I want to recount things without her . . . to wait for it to stop raining so that I can go to school, or, if the rain doesn't want to stop, then to take the red umbrella with tiny black dots from the hook in the kitchen and to leave. Some things we kept in strange places, even this habit reminds me of Mom, having plates in the guest room, and an umbrella in the kitchen, her customs were her life, her customs also became her death: in the hospital, in the ward that's visible from our balcony. To go outside, for me to go outside, and immediately be confronted by my mother's death, one hundred meters away, at times it's a ramshackle hut with five or six steps, at other times it's a ramshackle hut hidden among vegetation, weighed down by snow, a ramshackle hut with blossoming trees within reach, a ramshackle hut that sways in the wind . . . I take a pair of binoculars and she comes up to me, I look down the corridor through which people roam dressed in white robes, the room of my mother's death, first I see the room of her coma, and a moment later, here is also the room of her death with three empty beds. Mom is nowhere to be seen. Mom is buried on the hill, far away from there, but I know, I have a feeling that she's not inside her grave, rather, that first she's on one side, then on the other side of the hospital grounds—if I'm from here, she's from there, if I'm from there, she's from here, if I come, she goes, if she goes, I leave a moment before I see her . . . Begone plot, scram story, get out of my sight family home, let me put an end to myself with the language I breathe.

# ELIZABETA BAKOVSKA

## *The Yasnaya Polyana File*

BELIEVE ME, THERE were many times I wanted to hate you. None more so than when I threw our child into the Skopje sewer. The bloodied bundle that I ripped out of myself splashed into the water and was carried off downstream, somewhere far away from me, far away from my life back then. But you know nothing about that. Actually, you know nothing about many things. You know nothing because you never wanted to know. At that time, you came when you needed me, and left when you thought that I was no longer of any use to you. I knew it then, and I know it now: I was no more than an interlude in your life, a minor character, an additional source of inspiration for writing. But, I admit this freely now, regardless of whether you knew it or not, you were everything to me. My life was your brief visits, your whispered promises in those few moments of passion, the long waits for your appearance, and the hours I spent copying and rewriting what you'd written.

He came a few days later. He rang the doorbell, and when I opened the door, he greeted me politely, introducing himself and showing me his official ID. "May I come in?" he asked. I simply nodded yes. I was too exhausted to speak. He sat down at the kitchen table, and carefully pushed aside your scribbled manuscripts and my neatly typed corrected copies. With his index finger, he pulled a sheet of paper toward him and ran his eye over it. "You wrote this?" he said, and without waiting for my reply, he continued: "It's very good." He smiled at me when I opened my mouth to say something, and held up his hand. "Trust me, policemen read as well. I prefer the Russian classics. But this is really quite good." He remained silent a moment, and then in a low voice he said, "You should write for your own sake, in your own name. As things stand, he signs his name, they revere him, and what do you get out of it? Nothing!" We were sitting there in the kitchen. I didn't even offer him any coffee. I waited for him to tell me why he'd come. And he dived right into the most painful subject of all. He began talking to me about you. He said that you were just an average writer, even below average. "You know it's true," he added, smiling. "But you love him, don't you? You love him very much. That's why you offered to correct his stories and novels before they were published . . . Well, what's been published is much more yours than his." I wanted to get up. I wanted to tell him to leave. I wanted to say I don't know him and, for that reason, we have nothing to discuss about my life or you. I wanted him gone immediately, to be alone again, left to myself with the papers, with your words, with my words, with the stabbing pain in my stomach, with the desire to hate you. But I couldn't. I stayed seated opposite him while he told me everything. He told me that they'd been following you for months, and that they knew exactly when you'd come to visit me, and what we did. He told me where you went when you weren't here. He told me about your wife, about the children, about your drinking, about your arguments with other writers, about your sick ambitions. He told me everything I already knew or had sensed. And he even told me that he knows you'll never leave her and that you'll never be mine. "You frustrate him. You understand me, don't you?" he said to me kindly. "You write the way he'll never be able to write. And everyone thinks that it's he who writes like that. That's why he'll continue to come to you until he no longer wants to be a writer. And he'll never take you out in public; I mean to say, he'll never acknowledge you."

He offered me what you've never offered me—companion-ship. He told me that he'd come over once or twice a week for a chat, as friends, he stressed. Everything we talk about will remain between us, he said. What I tell him will be used purely for official purposes, just the bare facts, without names, without intimate details. He assured me, he swore, that no one would ever learn about us from him. He understood how alone I am with my hidden love for you, how much I need a shoulder to cry on at times. He doesn't judge anyone, he said. He knows what love is. He's felt it in his life, and not just toward his wife, but toward others as well. He told me he values those who love above those who hate, and he laughed at his own remark. He stood up and adjusted his shirt. Before he opened the front door, he turned toward me with both hands extended. He squeezed my hand, limp and cold from the stabbing pain in my stomach. "How are you, are you still bleeding?" he said with concern. He didn't give me a chance to reply. "It's not important how I know . . . If you need anything, I know a good gynecologist. Just call me." He put a slip of paper with a phone number on it in my hand and left.

From then on, he came over often. I lost count of how many times after a few years. We always just talked. We became good friends. Believe me, he never once tried anything else. Although, I don't know why I'm telling you all this, as if I'd sworn a vow of fidelity to you. He was a friend to me. A true friend. The only one who read me in your works. At times, especially in the beginning, he tried again to convince me that I should write in my own name, but then he gave up. Sometimes he brought over a hundred grams of pure Turkish coffee and we drank it together in the kitchen, with a box of Turkish delight. Sometimes he'd bring washing powder, and at other times flour, depending on what was in short supply at the supermarket. You never asked me where I got the coffee, as you sipped it with relish on the balcony, hidden behind the low wall in case anyone recognized you. You never asked me how I came by the washing powder, as you wiped yourself off on the clean bed sheets. And there was no need for you to pull out before you came. The gynecologist that had been recommended to me said that I'd never be able to have children again. But you didn't know that. The way you don't know many things, because you've never wanted to know.

Believe me, despite everything, I've loved you all these years. I still love you. I love you so much that if I could, I'd give you my pen and my thoughts and my words so that they might be truly yours, and not just signed by someone. I love you so much that I swallowed your lies without a word. I crumpled up my expectations with all your terrible stories. I tore them into the tiniest pieces, and threw them in the bin at night so that no one would see me. I love you so much that I never told you a thing about our only, unborn child. And I never wrote you anything besides this letter, which you'll receive tomorrow, hopefully before the journalists begin calling you. I'm not signing it with my own name, but with the one that my friend gave me, the one who swore that he'd never tell anyone about our talks. Frankly, I'm not surprised that he wrote down every one of my statements. I even felt somewhat flattered. I smiled when I read what he'd called me in your file. And yesterday, over his grave, I wept for my loneliness, and for that small bloodied bundle from thirty years ago. However, I don't expect anything from you. Nor do I want to bind you to me with these three or four pages that I'm writing to you. I just felt a need today to tell you how it was, because from tomorrow, everyone will know about me. No one will ever read you in the same way, and you, my dear, won't be able to choose not to know.

Forever yours,
Sophia Andreevna Tolstoy

# KALINA MALESKA

## *The Nonhuman Adversary*

MIRON ARONIEVSKI SAT down in front of his laptop and opened the document for translation. The repetitive, monotonous sound of his keystrokes and the blank expression on his face made it impossible to tell whether he enjoyed what he was reading or whether he found it painfully boring. Nevertheless, he applied himself to his task with assiduity. He'd open the document in English, and at the top of the page of the same document, he'd begin the translation into Macedonian. At the end of every paragraph he translated, he would delete the original text, thus reducing the number of paragraphs that remained to be completed. He approached all translation tasks the same way—surrounded by reference books, and making use of online dictionaries. He breezed through the pages in front of him with little difficulty, and the text being translated would retreat behind the letters of the language into which he was translating. One by one, the paragraphs from the original text disappeared, replaced by the translated paragraphs.

One day, Miron Aronievski sat down in front of his laptop, opened the document for translation, and saw that the text was 200 pages long. As usual, he placed the cursor at the top of the page and began typing in the necessary sentences. He deleted the first paragraph of the original text once he'd translated it into Macedonian. He did that for five pages, working well into the night. Exhausted, and barely able to see the letters in front of him anymore, he decided to turn off his computer and go to bed. Satisfied with his work, he looked down at the bottom left corner of the screen to check the page count: 200, and to confirm (although he already knew the answer, but he still liked to make sure) how many pages were left: 195. But lo and behold, the text had increased to 205 pages and he had a sudden sinking feeling that he hadn't progressed beyond the start.

He immediately came to life. He scrolled down to the last page to make sure that what he'd seen wasn't an illusion. The page number of the last page was 205. He thought that he might have gotten it wrong when he first opened the document, that the text had in fact been 205 pages in length all along, and that he had incorrectly remembered the number as 200. Well, fine, he thought. Regardless of this, he had still translated five pages, so that left 200. But when he downloaded the document again from the email, he saw that he hadn't been mistaken at all. The document for translation was 200 pages long. So, then, how could it have increased with the translation?

Miron Aronievski was worn out. He decided to go lie down and take his mind off this unpleasant incident. Tomorrow, he'd go at the translation hammer and tongs, and in no time bring it down to 190 pages.

Indeed, the next day Miron sat down in front of his laptop, mercilessly pounding out words on his keyboard, and the original text began to melt away. Every paragraph translated into Macedonian meant one further paragraph deleted from the original text, one less paragraph to translate. He was on page 15: that meant he had another 190 to go because the document was 205 pages long. He looked at the bottom left corner of the screen: the total number of pages had increased to 215.

Miron leaped off his seat as if jolted by an electric shock. He went to get a few reference books that he thought might be useful. He returned to take another look. The number 215 was still there, pitilessly displayed on the screen. He got up again. He had a drink of water, straightened a picture hanging crooked on the wall, moved his cell phone to another shelf, and checked whether his pen was still working. When he went back to his laptop, there in the bottom left corner of the screen the number 215 remained. The lines of the text were barely legible and looked like arrows pointing downward, as if they were laughing at him. Miron instinctively reached out by hand to try to straighten them. But touching the screen made no difference to the text. Then he closed the document and opened it again—the text was still 215 pages long.

Okay then, 215 it is. He decided not to pay any attention to this fact, and continued typing away at his normal pace. He pounded, flattened, and melted away the original text. After translating another five pages, he looked down at the bottom left corner of the screen, hoping that with twenty translated pages so far that would mean he had only 195 left. But there on the status bar stood the number 220. He'd translated 20 pages, but he still had 200 left. Miron closed his laptop without shutting down any of the programs, got up, and went out.

Over the next few days, he attempted to outmaneuver the text in any way possible. When instead of 200 pages he saw that there were 199 left, he would know that he had succeeded. Even if it meant ten days' work, he would make it to page 198. And even if it took a whole year, in the end he would translate the whole text. But whenever he checked to see which page he was up to and how many pages he had to go, there were always 200 pages left—this fact never changed.

Miron hammered away furiously at the keyboard, his greasy hair standing on end, his bloodshot eyes protruding from their sockets, and his cheeks sagging like a deflated balloon. Miron typed nonstop—his fingers developed muscles stronger than the biceps of swimmers, but he didn't get up from his seat in front of the laptop. The speed with which his fingers flew over the keys created a breeze that stirred all the loose papers on his table, swirling them around like a small whirlwind and sending them floating around the room. He was convinced that with his remarkable speed, in the end he would outwit these heartless numbers, and that he would cunningly melt away the text of one page from this document. After that everything would be easier. He would hammer, pound, flatten the paragraphs from the original, and recast them into the letters and words of his language. He typed day and night, surpassing all previous records for speed. But no matter how many pages he completed, there always remained 200.

When he reached page 200 and saw that the number at the bottom left corner of the screen was 400, in a fit of anger, Miron dived into his screen through a portal that had opened to receive him.

*

Miron Aronievski is still wandering through the regions of the text to this day. The text is hammering, pounding, flattening him, and Miron is slowly disappearing, getting smaller, melting away. He's so small that he's now turned into a letter. And he's still barreling forward through the pages as he continues to get smaller, afraid that he might disappear for good before he gets to the end of the text. But the end is nowhere in sight. Each time Miron succeeds in getting to the last page, the text expands by another page.

# SNEŽANA MLADENOVSKA ANGJELKOV

## *Menka*

IF THERE WAS one person we were scared to death of, it was definitely Menka. She had a tight perm that hung around her face in greasy curls. We were convinced that she owned only two dresses, because that's all she ever wore—a blue one with red flowers, and a red one with blue flowers that buttoned down the front, similar to a school uniform. In the wintertime, we never saw her outdoors. Instead of sending their young children to preschool, the neighborhood women, for an unspecified fee, would often leave them at Menka's place, because she'd previously worked as a preschool teacher. We thought it strange that the mothers were prepared to take such a risk, given Menka's bizarre methods of child-rearing, with which they were all too familiar. For example, some of the older children who attended the preschool said that she pushed their faces into their plates of food so they'd eat faster, while the boys said that she threatened to set their willies on fire with matches if they peed their pants. This image was engraved in our minds: Menka crouched down beside a boy with his underpants down around his ankles, her left hand tugging his willy, a burning matchstick in her right hand, paralyzing the poor little wretch with fear. We wondered what on earth she'd done to her husband, Uncle Risto, who spoke like a robot, holding one hand against his throat.

"Do—you—want—some—coff—ee?" he'd ask us whenever

we walked past the bench on which he often spent his mornings. We'd nod our acceptance. And he'd lean to one side, lift up one butt cheek, and let out a loud fart, which immediately sent us scattering.

"To—your—good—health!" he'd add, breaking into spurts of laughter.

One sweltering summer afternoon, the girl from Galičnik and I were fishing out earthworms from an ankle-deep puddle that had formed in the dirt path near a public water tap. We placed them down on dry ground so they could compete in a crawling race, while at the same time arranging leaves and twigs in front of them as obstacles. They stretched out and squeezed in their bodies like accordions, trying to evade our sticks, searching for holes to hide in. We waited until they crawled halfway into the hole, and then dragged them out again, prolonging their agony.

"Don't play with water, you'll pee your pants," Menka said, walking past us.

We didn't pay any attention to her and, as usual, we kept our heads down so that she wouldn't remember our faces and, God forbid, cast a spell on us so that we really did end up peeing our pants. The appearance of her son, Vance, lagging behind her, made our skin crawl. Even though he was a lot older than us and had already gone through puberty, he had zits all over his face, hands, back, even his ears! He was totally gross. That's why we ran as fast and as far away from him as we could, calling out to him, "Vance with the dry hands!" To tell the truth, he was quite tall and his hands swung at his sides like a pair of oars, so this rhyming taunt made sense. But more importantly, it was a good cover for the real reason for our flight. To scare us a bit, he sprang toward us, but then quickly gave up his intention, because he knew that we were as swift as arrows and that he would never be able to catch us. Or else he just left the dirty jobs to his mom, who suddenly appeared behind us out of nowhere and grabbed us by the hair.

"Why are you teasing my son?" Menka asked, lifting us off the ground, her eyes flashing angry sparks.

"Let go of us, Menka. We won't call him those names any-more." We squirmed like mice caught in a trap.

"I won't let you go. I'm going to lock you up in the cellar until you come to your senses."

The girl from Galičnik and I screamed as loud as we could. Perhaps out of fear, Menka quickly let us go, but with a warning that next time we wouldn't get off so lightly.

"You're gonna go over to Lozar Winery and get me some grape juice"—Vance ordered behind us—"and make sure the security guard doesn't see you. I'll give you ten minutes and then I'm coming after you. You know what'll happen if you don't do as I tell you."

We had no choice. We headed off to the winery, at the same time trying to think up a way to get through the wire fence with-out being caught red-handed. We skirted the perimeter of the warehouse. The only hole in the wire fence was near the crates filled with empty bottles.

"I'll get in from over there," said the girl from Galičnik. "You go to the other side and keep watch. If something happens, we'll meet out front of Slavija Supermarket."

Following her brief instructions, I ran over to the other side that faced the apartment buildings. The bottles of juice were peeking out of green crates covered by large sheets of paper with printed labels. I crouched down, trying to hide in the grass. Carefully, I stuck my arm through the wire mesh, but it got caught at the elbow. I wished I had Arabela's magic ring so I could shrink my body and squeeze through the wire, or other-wise be instantly transported home with a whole crate of juice. I tried stretching the wire by slowly twisting my arm from left to right. I even tried stretching it with my free hand, but without success. By this time my arm was swollen, and it could neither move backward nor forward. I heard someone call out to the security guard from the apartment building. I froze. My heart began to beat fast. It almost flew out of my chest.

"Here she is, over here," my archenemy continued calling out to the security guard.

Panicked and teary-eyed, with lightning speed I pulled out my arm that was throbbing and was slowly going numb. I screamed mutely and looked all around for the girl from Galičnik, but she was nowhere to be seen. I ran like crazy toward the supermarket, turning my head to look back a few times. I sat down on the windowsill and waited. The waiting turned into looking for a four-leaf clover in the small patch of grass in front of the super-market. Completely absorbed in my task, I didn't notice Vance and his zits approach. But I felt the force of the blow from his oar-like hand across the top of my head. It was so strong that I smacked the ground with my face, to which it seemed the time had come for me to return.

"Where's the juice?" demanded Vance, whose nickname from that point on would be Slimy Toad!

His face was dotted with bloodied scabs from freshly squeezed zits.

"I couldn't get any. The security guard came," I replied, want-ing to get as far away from him as possible so that I wouldn't catch his scabies.

"I'm gonna take you to my mom, who'll teach you a lesson, you little shit."

Vance grabbed me by the arm I'd injured trying to get through the wire mesh fence and pulled me after him, lifting me off the ground as if I were a little monkey. I begged him to let me go, but to no avail. At the corner of our apartment building, he stumbled awkwardly over an open manhole and, quick as a flash, I made a run for the entrance. I heard him cursing after me, but I paid no attention. Everything pained me. But what pained me most of all was the thought that the security guard at the winery might have caught the girl from Galičnik.

"Boo!"

I screamed. I almost peed my pants. The girl from Galičnik appeared at the entrance with two bottles of juice in her hand.

"Where've you been all this time?" I blasted at her angrily. "Look at what happened to me!" Tearfully, I showed her my arm, on which a bruise had started to show.

"I saw what he did to you. Come on, I've got a plan."

By the looks of it, the girl from Galičnik had been preparing revenge for quite some time. In an empty box of Turkish delight that she found on the bench in front of our apartment building, she placed some fresh horse dung and poked two sticks into it. We made our way over to the apartment building where Menka lived. We stood in front of her apartment and listened intently, pressing our ears gently to the door.

"They're home," the girl from Galičnik whispered. "They're about to have dinner."

We left the box filled with dung in their doorway, placed the two bottles of juice next to it, and ran outside. Underneath Menka's balcony, the girl from Galičnik began calling out at the top of her voice:

"Men-kaaaaa, Vaaaa-ance, there's some juice in front of your door. Enjoy your meal!"

We burst into giggles and headed back home.

"Now they'll come to their senses. They won't treat us badly anymore."

The excitement of our revenge was short-lived, lasting barely a few seconds. In the next moment, Vance was behind us. We ran toward the shopping mall, because we knew there'd be nowhere to hide at home. It was as if he was propelled by a rocket. He was getting closer and closer. We went down into the basement, the site for the proposed market, and hid inside the empty stalls that had been set aside there. The girl from Galičnik in one, me in another. We listened to Vance calling in a cracked voice for us to come out, and banging on the stalls with his hands. At one point, everything went silent. All I could hear was the rapid beating of my heart and the sound of my gasps as I struggled to take in air. My ears pricked up, straining to hear if Vance might have given up his search. A loud bang from a kick on the sheet-metal door released the floodgates in my bladder. I peed uncontrollably in the stall, shaking with fear. I heard Menka's voice approaching in the basement.

"Here she is, Mom!" Vance called out, holding the stall door shut.

When Menka arrived, she opened the door wide. I began to

scream at the top of my lungs. The whole basement echoed, as if with the screams of the inmates of concentration camps. Menka jumped back in fright, turned to face Vance and, pointing at me, said: "This one here won't be making any more trouble." She left the stall door open and went off. I just sat there exhausted, immobile in the stall. I felt like an earthworm immersed in its own puddle, from which the sour smell of urine began to spread.

# BERT STEIN

## *"Seventh Son of a Seventh Son"—Iron Maiden (1988)*

NINETEEN EIGHTY-EIGHT WAS A year of heavy metal. I'm not talking about the quality of the local drinking water, which probably no one in Yugoslavia monitored at that time. We trusted everything we consumed and everything we took in through our five senses, there was no doubt it was good—as long as it was ours. But, okay, I admit there were those who didn't believe quite so blindly in Yugoslavia. And with good reason too—the times were heavy, and getting heavier, just like the music.

At the time when heavy metal entered my life, wearing patches was popular. I didn't know the names of half the bands, but their logos—skeletons, skulls, guns, guitars—seemed to me sufficient reason for them to find their way onto my denim jacket. However, I did know Iron Maiden and I liked them. Their epic themes, rousing rhythms, and soaring vocals speak perfectly to young souls who are insecure and looking for their place in the world. Those patches often brought me trouble.

"Hand over your money!" The members of the gang known as "Korea" that operated in the area around the World War II memorial and the Sarajka Shopping Center ambushed Hare and me. I gave the impression of being a tough guy, which I actually wasn't, and that's probably what provoked them. But maybe they attacked me because they didn't take kindly to the idea of my having satanic heavy metal logos and standing near the war memorial. It insulted their almost Oriental sense of propriety. But unfortunately, they didn't reveal their political leanings— pro-communist or pro-American—as they were busy kicking my teeth in. Jokes aside, they beat me up for money, and when that's up for grabs, all sense of propriety becomes secondary.

There were many times I wanted to believe I was a street kid, because in one sense I think I really was. After the death of my grandmother, my grandfather withdrew into himself and I lost my most loyal companion. He spent most of his time at the War Veterans' Club, a sacred place for those who'd served in World War II, where they played bowls and cards. My grandfather would almost inevitably lose these games. Much later, I found out they could see his cards in his photochromic lenses, the type that darkened automatically beneath the bare bulbs in the club's smoke-filled rooms.

Who knows, maybe that was just something my father made up out of envy, because everyone knew my grandfather to be a "human calculator"—he could multiply large numbers quickly without batting an eye, and he could spot a mistake in rows of digits without the aid of a computer. But above all, like a magician, he always managed to find four-leaf clovers, which he would then give to me. All he needed to do was look in a clover meadow and he'd find one!

However, after he ended up alone, he was only a shadow of his former self. This new grandfather got angry at me for no reason, threw ashtrays at me, but he also knew how to protect me from the wrath of my father, who was disappointed at being twice divorced, and whose children were scattered God only knows where.

He smoked three packs a day, while for me it was like smoking one pack a month—taking into account the passive smoke I inhaled. But every now and then, I would light one up as well, if only to try and capture its luring effect. One day I was sitting alone, in front of me a cigarette and a lighter, beside me an empty glass. I lit up and took a drag. The taste, which I couldn't define, but which I'd later compare to burning metal and rubber, made my mouth fill with saliva. It just began to secrete like crazy. That's what the glass was for. I spat and puffed. It was disgusting, but I had to go through with it. It was a necessary part of growing up alone.

I grew up on the street with all of its rules. Although, I wasn't a lout, I never have been. My gentle exterior prevented me from becoming one; besides, I was fiercely loyal to my friends and to the group. I'd never betray them, not for anything in the world. I'd give them everything I owned—and sometimes I did. Every leather soccer ball my father brought back for me after attending medical seminars in Europe, I unselfishly shared with the other members of our group, every tennis racket, every tennis ball— and I always ended up with nothing. All of them got lost in the bushes on the slopes of our street in hilly Sarajevo. And sometimes the shiny, colorful leather soccer balls quickly ended up just becoming plaid patchwork. But that's how we all lived—not recognizing private ownership and dedicated to the common good. And if anyone violated that unwritten rule—well, tough luck to them.

The group went silent and the dancing stopped immediately. We were celebrating Vedo's birthday at his place, and everything was going great. The capitalist Coca-Cola went perfectly with the socialist pretzels that we mixed in our glasses, producing an exciting, frothy chemical reaction. We were listening to music, and then as a counterpoint to the seriousness and epic greatness of my favorite song, "Seventh Son"—"Push It" by Salt-N-Pepa came on the cassette player, a plain, simple, infectious, playful, sexual song . . . everything that heavy metal wasn't was in that song, which I thought sounded totally wicked, and so I was ashamed of myself. But that wasn't the reason for the shock. The silence came after one of our friends looked under the bed to retrieve a pretzel, and dragged out a brand spanking new tennis racket, unused tennis balls, uninflated soccer balls, and God knows what else! The spirit of sharing had been betrayed. I never looked at Vedo the same way again, and from that moment on I was quite reserved toward him.

But the group as a whole didn't change. It always found ways to move forward, to forget, to restore its energy through games, through coming up with new rules and new ways of playing. Vedo decided to share some of his tennis balls with us. We welcomed his initiative by gathering a few potato sacks and tying them together into a tennis net. The game continued.

It seemed that the group as a whole always lived according to the spirit of another popular song at the time, "Don't Worry, Be Happy," while at the same time the world was slowly preparing for the collapse of the Soviet Union and the fall of socialism. Yugoslavia was trying to maintain its own self-governing socialism, and failing miserably. "Be Worry, Don't Happy," as Rambo Amadeus would say many years later. Everything became more pressing.

The economic reforms of 1988 as a last-ditch effort for recovery of the virtually collapsed Yugoslav economy did not succeed. Even then signs began to appear that the nationalist and socio-economic uncertainties in Yugoslavia would lead to a state of emergency, but we were completely unaware of it.

To us kids, Yugoslavia was indestructible and more powerful than ever before. As for the economy . . . we knew how to deal with that as well.

Yasser was celebrating his birthday with a circus theme and, in the spirit of the new socio-capitalist times, he invited us to take part by performing some sort of an act. As the most jovial and the most inventive member of the gang, Hare immediately accepted. He put on a clown act in which he stumbled about, performed a pantomime, rode a bike hands free while falling over multiple times. We rolled around in hysterics.

"And now," Yasser announced theatrically, with a look of pure satisfaction on his face at the success of his self-organized circus (which at the time Yugoslavia itself actually was), "I invite you to take part in a competition!" We were all flabbergasted. The word "competition" echoed in our heads like a promise in the form of a sweet delicious lollipop, a shiny new toy, or the soccer and tennis balls we dreamed about. Instead, Yasser explained that we had to buy a ticket to win. We cried foul.

"On every ticket," Yasser continued without hesitation,

"there's a number. And each number corresponds to a toy." Hope returned to us. Wary, but tempted by the chance of winning something nice, we gave him the money. The first few tickets had no winners, but we'd come to learn that all games of chance were like that—you win some, you lose some.

And in fact, Hare won a shoddy toy truck that badly needed a new coat of paint; Fatty was delighted by the half-used notebook with Smurfs on the cover; and I won a toy Red Indian with one of his arms broken off. Several of the others won similar prizes, but then again, it was better than nothing—which is what a lot of them ended up with. The group wasn't happy. Serious arguments erupted over who got what, and whether Yasser had cheated us. He defended his entrepreneurial spirit, and told us that such was our luck.

Then his mother appeared, a strict but fair-minded woman of whom Yasser was deathly afraid, like fire. When she found out what he'd done, she gathered up all our old, shoddy toys, and brought out a box with newer and much nicer toys. She marked them with numbers and made tickets where there were no losers, bar one—her own son, who for the whole time sat with arms folded and a frown on his face, while the group thanked their lucky stars.

Yasser was ahead of his time. He was the embodiment of what many years later would become commonplace in all the former-Yugoslav republics—brute capitalism, a transition without end in which all are left to fend for themselves and survive as best they know, lying, cheating, doing whatever necessary.

The state no longer protected us, and it didn't actively discourage those who wanted to do harm, it didn't put a damper on their dirty dealings, and it didn't give the losers a second chance.

I fared better than my friends—I survived the breakup of my home and, with the death of Yugoslavia, I got a mother. But, overnight, people became orphans abandoned to the winds of time.

# ŽARKO KUJUNDŽISKI

## *Story Addict*

I NEED A story. I need it badly. You can't imagine how desperately I need one. Frankly, just between you and me, I'm as hungry for stories as an Andalusian dog. I'm not particular about how I come by them. Every day I enter into the lives of others—I delve deeply, draw them out, unearth things, expose them—I want every minor detail of their lives, the whole story.

My father buys me all the daily papers, all the weekly magazines. I can't live without the gossip columns and the crime and murder stories. I'm a lectiophile, I live for stories, I live off their remnants. I consume five hundred and seventy-four stories per week. That's my weekly dose. My grandparents find me annoying. I know all their stories and I force them to learn new ones. I demand they introduce me to their older and younger friends who know stories: folktales, their own stories, what they've read, what they've invented, all kinds . . . I can't do without stories. Tell me a story or I'll die!

Lie to me if you have to, but just tell me a story, tell me. Don't stop! Reveal your deepest, darkest secrets, your most morbid thoughts, your happiest events, your most unimaginable days. I want to know everything! Don't avoid the topic. Don't change the subject. It's not fair. I'm as quiet as a mouse, I won't say anything. I'm as silent as the grave. I can keep mum. People say: perhaps you should write. I reply: maybe. Someday. Not now.

But I know that'll never happen. I'm not a writer. I like to listen, to read, to fill up on a bunch of juicy, tasty, delicious, mouthwatering stories. About love, about death, about humanity, about murder, about fraud, about angst, about infidelity, about aliens, stories about history, about the present, about the future, about the well-known, about the little people. Tell me anything you like! Anything!

I'm all ears. I listen to all kinds of nonsense. No one else would do that, even if you paid them. I listen, I read, I'm a sucker for all kinds of stories. Before, I'd fall into depression or jump for joy when listening or reading. Today less so. You're wondering—why don't stories affect me like they used to? I've become a jerk, a heartless person, narrow-minded, a boor! How I hate what I've become! I want all the stories to make me feel sad or to cheer me up. I want them to touch me, to perk me up, to make love to me. I want them to captivate me, to feed me, to turn me into a story.

Give me matter, material, substance, stuff. Tell me about the woman who died of suffocation after falling into a manhole, about the old woman combing her hair while her village burned, about the man who—naked and barefoot—defied the bullets, about the child who saw flying saucers, about the young man who jumped off a building from the twelfth floor. Call me at home, on my cell phone, try me at work. Let the boss tell me off, let him fire me. Just give me an exciting story. I want to break down when you tell me: it happened like this. I want to tremble. I want my heart to clench, my throat to close up. After that—to be unable to speak. Ring me! I'll duck under the desk. I'll just listen—you tell me, tell me, tell me . . . I'll keep quiet. I won't interrupt you. It's happened to me many times before. My colleagues thought I was drooling over the phone, carrying on some sort of intimate conversation on goodness only knows what sort of topic. But, no, I often find myself firmly holding the handset, while you over there, on the other side of the line, tell me, tell me, tell me . . .

What a wonderful feeling! Tell me a story! I'd do anything for a good story. I'd go down twenty thousand miles below sea, I'd climb the Himalayas, I'd travel unaccompanied through western

Macedonia. For a good, powerful story, I'd give up my name, my family, my past, my future, I'd give up Ireland like Joyce . . .

I'm an ideal listener. All stories are made up just for me. All novels are written for me. I'm the best friend of anyone who wants to tell a story. I don't know what I'd do if stories didn't exist. Probably I wouldn't exist either.

"I listen and read, therefore I am" is my motto. I swallow novellas for breakfast, I eat whole tomes for lunch, I snack on short stories and fall asleep with epics on my mind. But, no, I'm telling a lie—I don't sleep at all. I spend the night in the attic, with a candle, like Kočo Racin, with books, with letters from acquaintances and unknown people, with their stories. I get letters from everyone. Now I'll send my message off into space. I'll write it on the lunar surface. I want to be the first to receive a message from another planet, the first to relay it. I already have that exclusive story from another world, but I'll tell you about it some other time. It's not important to me at this moment. What's important is that if I don't get a story in the next five minutes, if I don't hear something, if I don't read something, I'll fall ill, and I'll lie ill for nine years. Dammit, let me fall ill, just as long as my eyes and ears still serve me.

I know the librarians in all the libraries, the booksellers in all the bookshops and street stalls. People panic when they see me approach. They chase me off. Because of me they can't close their shops. Several times the police came and removed me forcibly. They grabbed me by my collar and dragged me off. I'd kneel down before them saying: you must have a lot of things to tell. Tell me, I beg you, tell me about someone who became an insect, about the purloined letter, about the man who died in Venice, about the strand of hair that got washed down the bathroom sink . . .

On three occasions at night, I've smashed several bookshop windows in order to get my hands on the new books they didn't tell me about during the day. I've been threatened with prison time twice. I've come as far as going to jail. Nice work! In fact, tonight I'll smash another window, because prisons have amazing libraries with lots of books, and not many people who read there. I'll do it tonight. I'll steal some books from the nearest bookshop. I'll take as many as I can so I can receive a long sentence. I have to do it! I'm ready. I feel dizzy. I feel faint. Stoooooooooory. Give me a story!

I know English, French, and Russian. I'm also going to start learning Chinese, Hindu, Arabic, and Bengali. I want to know all the languages, to read everything that exists. Will I have enough time, because, according to statistics, the Macedonian male has a life expectancy of seventy years? Therefore, I have thirty-nine years left. If I read fifty pages per hour for twenty hours per day, that makes it a thousand pages per day. How little that is! I have to read faster, to waste less time on unimportant things—eating, drinking, sleeping. I have to find a faster way of getting my hands on books, not losing precious time searching for call numbers, going to libraries, providing listings, extorting narratives.

I even got divorced. At night my wife constantly tickled my stomach, while I just read and read and read. When I came home early in the morning, with clothes that looked as if they hadn't been ironed in months, she grew suspicious of me. She thought that I'd been out God only knows where, doing God only knows what, when in actual fact I was returning from parlor gatherings of women complaining about their daughters-in-law, from get-togethers of drunk men singing their own praises, from support group meetings for single mothers and victims of domestic violence.

Well then, now that you know me better, look out for me. I'm easily recognizable—wherever I go, I wear a helmet like the one worn by Don Quixote, my beloved hero. If you come across me at a café, cinema, theater, library, don't think twice—I'll immediately hear your confessions. If you're a born storyteller, I'm a born listener. Don't worry, you'll figure out who I am without any problem. It's not difficult to spot a story addict.

This is the first time I've ever written anything. This is not a story. This is an ordinary account, a letter written in agony. Will somebody please tell me a story? There must be someone who doesn't read, who just writes. I'm searching for my ideal storyteller, someone who'll tell me stories non-stop. I'll just listen or just read what they write. But that's worse because they can't write as fast as I can read. They'll have to read aloud to me and I'll listen. I'm looking for someone like that. Call me. Call me at once. Right away!

Indeed, a thousand pages for three hundred and sixty-five days per year, that's three hundred and sixty-five thousand pages per year. Oh, three hundred and sixty-five thousand pages times thirty-nine years, that's a total, more or less, of fourteen million, two hundred and fifty thousand pages to the end of my life. Nooooo! That's merely a dozen shelves of books in an ordinary school library! I can't end up like Byron. I can't end up going blind like Borges. I can't end up becoming a vagrant like Rimbaud, becoming unhinged like Poe. Why aren't I a woman? They live longer than men. Imagine if I were a woman born in Iceland! Exactly eighty-three years of life! Madness. But don't think that I'm afraid of death. I would gladly die if I knew that after that they would tell me a great story, a story to end all stories.

Ugh! I'll definitely give up the ghost if I don't read something in the next five minutes. The phone hasn't rung once all day, and I don't have another book at hand. I want something new. I've already read everything I have at home. My father should've been back by now. He should've brought me back some fresh stories. I could reread something, but I don't want to. That way, I'll forever be beyond my desire to read everything. Oh, I feel so empty, so poor, so hungry!

They won't even let me outside anymore. A decree was issued by the authorities. Apparently I pose a danger to the community. Apparently I peer through people's windows, I listen in on them, I open their mail, I stick my nose into people's personal business. They treat me like a criminal. And all I do is read and listen to stories. Is there anything wrong with that? I'm an ordinary reader. I'm not a thief, a thief of stories. I know all the stories from Adam and Eve to the boyish skirmishes in our streets.

I'll take my suitcase full of nothing and go around the world in search of stories. Sad, happy, funny, boring, short, long, old, modern, beautiful, foreign, fantastic, unreal, surreal, real, all kinds of stories. Jokes, anecdotes, sagas, travel stories, tales, fables, legends . . . Stories! Stories! I'm buying stories! I'm buying, buying, buying stories! Old, new, all kinds! I run down the street yelling: I'm buying stories! I'm not some sort of agent, an exploiter of rights. I believe that all stories belong to everyone. Nobody owns stories. There are so many similar, almost identical stories in the world, so we can't say that someone stole from another. I, for one, don't have any stories of my own. My story is just a patchwork of all the stories that I've read and heard.

What is this? What's happening, I'm carrying on a bit, this isn't normal, I'm getting carried away, I've been talking too long, I'll forget to listen, I'll forget to read, give me new stories, tell me a story! Time's running out, my breath is failing me, is the story addict in me really dying? Where's my father? He's late. The phone hasn't made a sound. What's up with all these people? The newspapers publish the same news. The mailbox is empty. Hurry up, ring, write, tell me, find me! I'm dying for a story. Act while there's still time. You mustn't keep me apart from my undying love. That's exactly what you're trying to do. This is a conspiracy against me. But, behold, I make a vow, I swear that in good times and bad, in happiness and misfortune, I love and will always love stories, and only stories! Now and forever, into eternity.

By His Own Hand,
Ognen Ljameski

*This letter (with the exception of a few interventions on my part, mainly the clarification of names) arrived at the editorial office of the daily newspaper Dnevnik on July 24, 1999, where, at the time, I happened to be in a meeting with the then Chief Editor, Mr. Aleksandar Damovski. Knowing my fondness for literature, he handed the letter to me. I probably would have just filed this piece of paper away somewhere if, in an analysis of print media that began for entirely different reasons, and by my own deductions, I hadn't noticed the connection of this letter with three other very interesting events.*

*On August 17, 1999, several daily newspapers published the news that a group of children had discovered a medieval knight's*

helmet encased in mud by the Vardar River, close to the Katlanovo
Hot Springs. The owner of the helmet is unknown. Today that helmet is held in the secret vaults of the Museum of Macedonia, because
displaying it to the public could give rise to further, unnecessary
nonsense in world history.

On September 21 of that same year, ERT TV in Greece reported
that two mailbags disappeared overnight from the post office in
Monemvasia, southern Greece. Five days later, the letters were deliv-
ered to their respective addresses by an unknown person.

The third piece of news, probably the strangest, and perhaps the
least closely tied with this event, was dispatched by all foreign news
agencies a few years later, on June 13, 2001. It stated that, with the
aid of the TM198 electric telescope, for the first time ever a group
of astrophysicists had noticed hieroglyphic signs on the surface of the
moon. Precise analysis later confirmed they weren't hieroglyphics,
but Cyrillic letters.

In the hope that I have made my humble contribution to the
search for the curious author of the letter, the self-styled story addict,

Yours,
I. M.

# RUMENA BUŽAROVSKA

## *Lily*

LILY WAS NOT a pretty girl. I'd known that ever since she was born. She was quite a hairy baby, very dark. She was born with bushy hair, with eyebrows that almost met over her nose and that never thinned out. Her eyes were quite small, but over time they began to gleam. She had long, delicate little fingers and toes, with curved and shiny nails that were never sharp, even when I cut them. Jovan kissed them all the time. Although he would have preferred a son, when he saw Lily, his face lost all its authority, all its sternness, becoming round and soft. His eyes misted over whenever he saw her. He'd take careful hold of her little fingers and toes, gently kiss them and nuzzle his face in them. *Liliana, Lily, Lilikins*, he cooed while kissing her.

She was meant to be called Petra, after my mother, and if we'd had a son he'd have been named Risto, after Jovan's father. But Jovan started calling her Lily, after his mother, when he first laid eyes on her, and we never discussed the issue of her name any further. Lily stayed Lily, after his dead mother.

Jovan didn't like my mother at all. She reminded him of poverty and illness. After my father died, she lived alone in the village, poor and quite sick. She couldn't get up out of bed. We sent money to my brother, and he and his wife went to see her and looked after her as much as they could. The rest of the time she just lay there alone with a sour smell that clung to her, the smell of slow death. Every now and then a neighbor went over to help her. Jovan wouldn't let me go and look after her. That's why he regularly sent money for her instead. Before Lily was born, I'd wait until he was away on business and then I'd take the train to her place. I'd bake her some bread, cook her something, stroke the back of her bony hands, kiss her forehead, and take the last train back home at night. Whenever I showed up there, the neighbors shot daggers at me. They looked at me as if I were some kind of murderer. My brother stopped liking me as well, and his wife refused to have anything to do with me.

Jovan found out once that I'd left the house when I was pregnant. "Do you want to get sick?" he yelled, even though my mother wasn't suffering from anything contagious. "Do you want to kill my child?" he shouted, turning red with rage.

Since Lily was born, I've never managed even once to take her to my mother's so she could see her. I waited for Lily to spring up and start walking, so that we could sneak off to the village when Jovan was away on business. But Lily was a bit slow. She started walking late, and when she did start, she walked like a young fawn. She wasn't like the other children, with a strong, lumbering gait. Her steps were tentative, fearful, and she was frail. Jovan felt like crying whenever he looked at her, and the whole time he just carried her in his arms and kissed her. Then she'd laugh a little, although Lily didn't laugh much at all.

When we took her out for a walk in the stroller, the women in the neighborhood would stop to look at her, as they did with all the other little children. When she turned one, she didn't look like a girl at all. Her hair was still short, with thick black curls. She looked more like a boy. "May your little son live a long and healthy life," the neighborhood women would say. Jovan would get very angry. "She's a girl, her name's Lily," he corrected them. "Then put a hair clip on her so that people know she's a girl," shot back one of the bolder women.

When Lily turned one and a half, and she was walking more confidently, I decided to get her ears pierced. At first, I was afraid to tell Jovan. But he immediately approved because he felt slighted whenever people said that Lily was a boy, and when they didn't say that she was pretty. I took her to get her ears pierced. After that she cried for the rest of the day, and I with her, her little earlobes red and swollen. When Jovan came home, we were both exhausted from crying. Lily was hiccupping. I felt bad for hurting her, and was afraid of what Jovan would say. But he just took her in his arms, planting kisses on her face and on her fingers, and Lily calmed down.

A month later, I took out the earrings that her ears had been pierced with and replaced them with the gold earrings that my mother had given me when I last went to see her, back when I was pregnant. "Your belly is round like a ball, which means it's going to be a girl," she said to me, and gave me the gold earrings in the shape of flowers with red precious stones in the center. They were the earrings my mother wore when she was young. I remember hugging her and nuzzling into her neck, her earrings gently brushing against me.

Jovan came home and saw Lily's earrings. He smiled. "They're really beautiful," he said. "Did you buy them?" They were quite old-fashioned. I would have had to lie about where I got them, but I wasn't sure I could pull it off. What if he checked at the shop and discovered that they didn't sell that type of earrings there? "They're my grandmother's," I said. "Who gave them to you?" he asked. "My aunt gave them to me before she left for Australia," I lied. "They're very beautiful," he said once again. He touched Lily's earrings gently, and kissed her on the nose. I could hardly wait for Jovan to go away on business again. Then I could take Lily to my mother's so she could see her with the earrings.

It was September and we were making ajvar. I made it the way my mother had taught me. My sister-in-law's ajvar was never as good as mine, nor the one my mother used to make. I made it together with my friend, Kristina. Jovan didn't know how much ajvar we made. He also loved to eat it. He said it was the best ajvar he'd ever tried, even though it was based on my mother's recipe. I told him once that it was my mother's recipe and he didn't say a thing. He just kept eating.

Kristina and I were sitting out front of our apartment building, roasting and peeling peppers, stirring the ajvar, and chatting.

Lily was playing with Kristina's daughter on the lawn. Kristina's daughter was four years old. She treated Lily like a doll because Lily was slow and fragile, but Lily never cried or caused any trouble. Occasionally, we'd let them peel a pepper, or help them stir the mixture with the wooden spoon.

Kristina was a close friend, and knew about the situation between Jovan and my mother. I told her that I'd make some extra ajvar and that I planned to take at least six jars to my mother, something that Jovan didn't need to know. I also told her that Jovan was going away on business the following week, and that I was going to go to the village with Lily to see my mother. It would be the first time my mother ever saw Lily, I told Kristina, and Lily was going to wear my mother's earrings. My mother doesn't have long to live, I said to Kristina, watching the ajvar slowly bubbling.

Jovan was at work when we filled all the jars with ajvar, so he wasn't to know how many there were for us, and how many would be left over for my mother. I put the six jars that I'd set aside for her into a box, and the box into a plastic bag. The bag was quite heavy. Not only did I have to carry Lily and the box, but a bag with all of Lily's things. I didn't take the stroller because it would have meant extra weight. I carried Lily in one arm, propped against my hip, and her bag and the box with the ajvar in my other arm.

We got on the train last, barely managing to find a compartment with a free seat. There was nowhere for me to put my belongings, so a man helped me put the box and the bag with Lily's things in the rack above the seat. I sat Lily on my lap and we set off. Lily didn't cry, didn't complain. She played quietly with a toy—a little white lamb. When the compartment emptied out a bit a few stations farther on, I sat Lily on the seat next to me. Two elderly women were sitting opposite us. "What a sweet little girl," they commented. "Look at how quiet and well mannered she is. *Ptu-ptu-ptu*," they cooed, smiling at us. After that they started asking a lot of questions: where was my husband, did I work, where did we live, where was I going alone with the child. I didn't want to tell them anything because I was afraid they might be from the same or a neighboring village, and that word would get around that I'd come with Lily, and then Jovan might somehow find out that we'd gone to see my mother. I didn't know how to avoid their questions, so I just kept silent, which came across as rude. Soon the old women began staring suspiciously at me, with their jaws clenched in protest, casting curious glances at one another. They got off at the station before ours without saying goodbye.

We were left alone in the compartment with a man who dozed the whole time and who seemed rather unsociable. He was unshaven, unwashed, and stank of cheap salami. He was wearing a checkered jacket, which was frayed at the sleeves and had a large grease stain on the collar. Under his jacket he wore a jumper that had small holes around the neckline and a larger one at his gut. His hands were rough, and he had black dirt under his fingernails and in the wrinkles in his hands and palms. A couple of times he opened one eye and stared at us. When we arrived at our station, he got up and left the compartment without offering to help me.

I got up to get the box of ajvar and the bag with Lily's things from the baggage rack above. I stood on tiptoes and tried to drag the bag with the box of ajvar down toward me. Just as I thought I had it in my hands, the train suddenly jerked forward, sending me sprawling backward. I fell to the ground and saw the bag with the ajvar fall on top of Lily's head and then land on the ground. The box inside the plastic bag immediately broke open and I saw something red leak from it. Lily collapsed onto her side, lying over the armrest of the seat.

Her eyes were closed and she was unconscious. I began to shake her and call out her name. I checked her head and saw that there was no blood anywhere. After that Lily slowly began to open her little eyes. Her gaze was somewhat absent, unfocused. One eye seemed to be moving to the right while the other kept still. Then her mouth suddenly crumpled and she began to whimper softly. "Bam-Bam," she said, and grabbed her head. People passing through the carriage looked into the compartment, but no one stopped to help. I hugged Lily, lifted her into my arms, and grabbed the handles of the bag containing the box with the ajvar. It was very heavy and I realized that it would soon break. A red, oily liquid had gathered at the bottom of the bag from the broken jar.

I got off the train. Lily was whimpering. At times she would start crying louder, but then quickly quiet down, as if she didn't have the strength to cry. "Bam-Bam," she repeated, holding her head with her little hand. The bag was getting heavy in my left hand and I was leaving a trail of red oily spots in my wake. It was at least another fifteen-minute walk to my mother's house. As I was walking, the bag broke. I saw that two of the jars were broken. I left the jars, the box, and the broken bag on the side of the road. I put two jars into the bag with Lily's things, and the other two jars I held in my hand. It began to drizzle. My hands and feet were shaking, my back was stiff, and I was drenched in sweat. Several people passed me but I didn't say hello because it was as if I didn't see them.

We arrived at my mother's place. She was asleep with the television blaring. When we went into the house, the sound smacked me in the face and I turned the volume down because Lily was beginning to cry even louder. Inside the house it was dark and smelled moldy and sour. My mother was fast asleep, snoring lightly with her mouth open.

I sat down on the small wooden stool beside her and put Lily on my lap. I began feeling around Lily's head, gently pressing it to see whether it was sore, or if there was a bump, and if she was bleeding anywhere. But Lily didn't react. Her gaze was empty and it seemed to me as though one of her eyes was moving a bit to the right again. She whimpered and cried for a bit, then stopped. She would say, "Bam-Bam," then stop speaking. I thought about putting her to bed and placing an ice pack on her head, but then realized that my mother didn't have a freezer. And I didn't want to put Lily to bed in my mother's house that smelled of death. All I wanted to do was leave and take Lily home. I just wanted to lie down together with her, wake up the following day, and kiss her on her little nose and her little mouth. I'll never lie to Jovan again, I said to myself, and I'll never go to visit my mother ever again.

I wished that my mother were dead so that none of this would have happened. I looked at her snoring steadily with her mouth open. From it spread a stale, fetid, rotten stench. I looked at her and hated her for being alive, for not dying, for making me cause Lily harm. I had brought Lily here because of her, to this place that reeked of death.

I left the jars on the table, put Lily on my hip, and went out. I ran all the way to the station to catch the first train back. On one of the shabby benches on the platform that smelled of piss, I held Lily tightly and stroked her head. She had stopped whimpering, and was calm and breathing evenly. But she wasn't the same Lily. I could sense that, even though I couldn't say why.

Instead of going straight home when we arrived, I went to Kristina's. Her husband and her children were home. She was making pita. She was covered in flour up to her ears. She took fright when she saw me. Goodness knows what I must have looked like. She pulled me and Lily into the kitchen and closed the door.

Once the door was closed, I started crying. I held Lily tightly, but she was limp and showed no interest in anything. The whole time she looked sad and lost. Even when I began to cry it didn't seem to upset her the way it normally did whenever I cried or argued with Jovan at home. Now she just stared at me and let out a small whimper, so I cuddled her and she stopped. I told Kristina what had happened.

"You have to take her to the hospital," Kristina said to me, gently stroking Lily's short black curls.

"What do you mean take her to the hospital? Jovan can never find out about this."

Kristina kept silent. I was silent too.

"It's nothing," I tried to assure myself. "She's probably just suffered a slight concussion. I'll put her to bed early."

"Lily, Lily!" Kristina called out to her. Lily raised her head and looked toward her.

"Fine, it doesn't look as if it's anything serious. But she looks dazed. I don't know what to say to you. Perhaps you should still take her to the hospital."

"What do I tell Jovan? No matter whether I was at home alone, or at your place, it would still end up being my fault that Lily got hurt. He'll kill me. He can never find out."

Again Kristina said nothing and we both sat silently.

"Don't worry. You only see the bad side to things. Come on, it'll pass, she's a kid. Children are forever falling over and getting hurt then jumping up again," she said to me, trying to summon a smile.

"Yes, she'll get over it. It's nothing. Isn't that right, Lily? Does anything hurt, darling?"

"Bam-Bam," Lily said again, and grabbed her head.

We went back home and I thought it best to let Lily sleep and rest. I put her to bed and then lay down on my own bed, which was next to hers. Kristina had tried to calm me down when we were at her place, but it hadn't worked. I waited for Lily to fall asleep and when I heard her breathing steadily, I took a pill, then fell asleep.

I woke up around midnight. Jovan was standing over Lily's bed and he was kissing her. "My little ducky," he whispered, kissing her fingers. Lily flinched slightly, but stayed asleep. After that, Jovan lay down beside me and fell asleep.

Jovan's screams woke me in the middle of the night. He was screaming like a banshee, holding Lily in his arms and shaking her, but Lily wasn't moving. I managed to call the ambulance somehow, although I felt as if I were in a dream and I couldn't dial the numbers properly. After that we got into the ambulance and we all went to the hospital. It was daybreak when they told us that Lily had died. The doctors began to ask me questions. How was the child behaving the previous day? Had she fallen over or been hit by someone perhaps? I told them that everything was as usual, like every other day. I told them that Lily had hardly cried at all, nor had she behaved strangely. We'd been at home the entire day, and in the afternoon we'd gone to visit my friend— Kristina, I said, and glanced at Jovan. She behaved normally there as well, I told them.

The doctor asked us if Lily had had any health problems, and whether there were any hereditary diseases in our family. I shook my head no, while Jovan was biting down on his clenched fist and squeezing his eyes tight. "I had a brother who died of stroke when he was a baby," he said. I didn't know about that. The doctor simply nodded, and concluded that it was most probably due to this same cause.

Around midday I rang Kristina to tell her that Lily had died. I told her that the funeral would be held at noon the following day. And I told her that Jovan knew nothing. If anyone asks, Lily and I came to visit you in the afternoon and Lily was her normal self. "Okay?" I asked. Kristina said nothing. I heard her sniffling on the other end of the phone. I hung up because I didn't want to hear her crying.

It was particularly painful for me to look at Kristina and Jovan at the funeral. But they were around me the entire time, howling with grief. Kristina just kept staring at me with a fixed gaze, her mouth half-open and wet with spit, emitting a vague moan. She didn't even try to use a handkerchief so we wouldn't all have to stare at her slobbering mouth. Jovan wasn't himself and looked a terrible sight. The whole time he held on to my sleeve, pulling me down. I could barely stand upright myself anyway, and I felt like just getting down on the ground and crawling. I didn't need his extra weight. At one point we both tumbled over and the mourners broke out into a cry. Someone grabbed me from behind so roughly that it left two bruises on my arms. I tore my pantyhose and my feet got muddy because it had been raining all that day. Some stupid relative said that the heavens were crying for Lily and then just patted me on the back. A shiver of disgust ran down my spine.

After that, Jovan changed dramatically overnight. His face fell, his eyes became permanently teary. He went bald and gray. All that was left of his hair was a band around his scalp and a white tuft above his forehead. From a big solid man, he turned into a small and meek one. Even his demeanor softened, which disgusted me. He stopped going away on business trips so much, and began going to bed the same time as me, which kept me from falling asleep. He'd lie down beside me and hug me. He'd begin snoring as soon as he was asleep, and after a while he'd stop snoring and start tossing and whimpering and groaning. I'd wake him and he'd burrow even closer into me and start hugging and stroking me. He'd whimper quietly, and then fall asleep again. The first month I was too afraid to move or say a word. But I soon realized that I didn't have to be afraid of him. I kicked him out of our bed. "Please, just don't make me sleep in a different room," he pleaded. So we slept on separate beds in the same room.

After a time I noticed that he'd also begun to soften his attitude toward my mother. The first time he mentioned her, he said that Lily looked a bit like her. This observation seemed to me to be in poor taste as he was probably alluding to her eyebrows, which met above her nose. When Lily had been alive, he always said that she looked like his mother. Now all of a sudden, according to him, Lily began to look like my mother. That also galled me, but I didn't say anything. After a few days he mentioned her again, while we were having lunch. I had cooked a vegetable and meat stew. While chewing away, he said that I was the only person who could make such a delicious stew. Then he just swallowed and stared at me. His mouth was covered in grease because he never remembered to wipe his face with a napkin. "Your mother taught you to cook well. It's a pity that she got sick." Again I said nothing. "How's your mother?" he asked, cutting another thick slice of bread. I just shrugged my shoulders. I didn't feel like talking about my mother. I hadn't been to see her since Lily died, and her life was just an added burden on me. "Have you heard from your brother?" he continued to ask me. "No," I lied. My mother was the same as she'd always been. Sick, poor, and immobile.

But Jovan wanted to keep on talking about her. One day he suddenly asked: "When are we going to your mother's?" No doubt I gave him a puzzled look because his teary eyes widened visibly. He wanted to say something, but nothing came out. "I'll go alone," I said to him. But I didn't go, as I didn't want to. I was sick of my mother and of him, and at times I wished them both dead.

But Jovan didn't let up asking when we would go to my

mother's. "There's no reason for you to go to my mother's. You've never visited her before. She never saw Lily, and now you want us both to go. Don't mock her even further," I said to him.

He bowed his head so that all I could see was the tuft of hair. He was like an old child. "Okay, just go alone," he said to me. He took some money out of his pocket and gave it to me. There was quite a bit.

"Don't go by train. Take a cab instead," he said to me. "We have the money."

I took the money and the following day, after he left for work, I put it in my pocket and went out. I didn't want to go and see my mother. I headed toward the shopping center downtown. At one store I bought myself some leather gloves, from another a silk scarf. I could easily hide them until I told Jovan that I needed some money to buy a scarf and gloves. I put them in my bag. I could hardly wait to sit down somewhere so that I could admire them, feel how soft they were, savor their smell of newness. Then I decided to go to a restaurant. I sat down in a corner so that no one could see me. I didn't feel like eating, but I didn't have anything to do, and I'd never been to a restaurant alone before. For starters I ordered pindjur with bread and cheese, even though I wasn't hungry. But when the food arrived, the bread was warm and the cheese was soft and the pindjur refreshed me. After I'd eaten, I felt better. Then I ordered a burger with a side dish of boiled vegetables. I also ordered a glass of red wine. Before the food arrived, I unpacked the gloves and the scarf and smelled them, gently rubbing them against my cheek. I felt good. I didn't feel like crying anymore. That's when the food arrived and I ate all of it. I ordered baklava for dessert, and then an ice cream. I took out the gloves and the scarf once again and admired them. As I still had time, I went to the cinema. I didn't care what film I saw. It was some sort of historical film. I dozed off in the big theater chair and once the film finished, I went home.

"How's your mother?" Jovan asked me when he got home from work.

"The same as always," I said. Suddenly I burped up onions. I was worried the smell might give me away.

"What did you have to eat there?" he asked me, as if he knew what I'd been doing.

"I made her some hamburger patties with onion. I bought some meat before I went to see her." I was surprised at how quickly I made something up.

"Mmm, delicious," Jovan said, smiling at me. He then came over and gave me a big hug, while I just stood there like a pillar. "Go there again next week," he said to me.

"If you say so," I agreed.

\*

My mother passed away six and a half months after Lily died. It was a relief to me, but Jovan was visibly shaken. He followed me around and stared at me all the time. He'd ask me if I needed anything, make me coffee, buy me sweets, and the following day, without asking, he prepared dinner for us both. He paid for the funeral, the plot, and the gravestone, but I managed to persuade him that we needn't go to the funeral itself. I told my brother and my sister-in-law that we couldn't deal with another burial. They just sighed on the other end of the phone. Kristina also came over when she found out. Ever since Lily died, I'd been avoiding her.

We sat opposite one another in the kitchen, at the breakfast table. That was where I used to drink coffee with her and with my other friends, before Lily died. She was staring at me, sniffling and nervously picking at the skin around her fingernails.

"How are you?"

"All right."

"You've put on some weight," she said.

I didn't respond. I didn't care if I was fat or thin, and I didn't think it was any of her business. After that she started talking about my mother—what a lovely woman she'd been, what a hard life she'd had. She also said something stupid to try to comfort me, something along the lines of my mother having two children of whom she could be proud.

"What pride are you talking about, Kristina?" I couldn't help myself. "I left her lying sick at home and didn't go to see her for two years. When I went to see her with Lily, I didn't wake her up. She died without having seen her granddaughter. I didn't name my child after her."

"That's because of your circumstances," she said to me. "I'm sure she understood. Your father was a difficult man, too."

We both sat there silently. Suddenly she took my hand and squeezed it. I don't know how or why, but all at once I burst into tears. She started crying too.

"You've got to tell Jovan," she said.

"Tell him what?"

"Well, you know," she said.

"I've never heard anything more stupid," I replied. "Why should I tell him such a thing? Do you want me to die as well?"

"You'll die from your conscience. Secrets can eat at you from the inside," she said to me, and started crying again. "I have nightmares every night. I think that if you don't tell him, something terrible will happen."

"What could be worse than what's already happened? Stop talking nonsense."

"It's not fair on him. Don't you see how he's changed? All he does is run after you. As if he thinks it's his fault."

"It *is* his fault," I said to Kristina.

\*

When Jovan and I went to bed that night, before he fell asleep, I heard him crying from his bed. "What is it now?" I asked him.

"Forgive me."

"For what?"

"For your mother."

Silence fell between us.

"I was afraid of her illness. I thought that something might happen either to you or to Lily if you went to visit her. The thought of her and her house and her village and everything frightened and disgusted me. I wanted to take you out of all that."

I said nothing. He tried to steady his voice.

"But in the end Lily died because of me. Her illness came from my family. It's all my fault," he said, and burst out crying.

*It's your fault*, I wanted to say to him. *You're to blame, and no one else. It's your fault, your fault, your fault*, I kept saying to myself, while aloud I told him to stop talking nonsense, to let me get some sleep, and to stop giving me a hard time because it was *my* mother who'd died, not his.

\*

That night I dreamed that Kristina and I were sitting out in front of our apartment building, stirring ajvar. The ajvar was thick and unnaturally red. We were laughing and chatting like we used to. I liked being with Kristina and I felt relaxed around her. But then suddenly a hush came over the whole neighborhood. The quiet enveloped us. We fell silent and continued to stir the ajvar slowly. Our hands and nails were red from peeling peppers. It got harder and harder to stir the ajvar with a spoon. I looked at Kristina. Her eyes were red and swollen. I'm going to tell him, she said. I'm going to tell him, she repeated. You won't say anything, I said to her, and somehow I knew that my words would be hypnotic and that she would do whatever I told her to do. All of a sudden the spoon got stuck in the pot. I looked inside. The ajvar was glowing red and was as smooth as water. The spoon was caught on something. I could barely manage to lift it out. On the tip of the spoon were black, wet curls. I put the spoon back into the pot and then pulled out a black hair from my mouth. Just as I took it out, I felt that there was another one in there, and I pulled out a whole handful of curls. I looked at Kristina worriedly, but instead of her, opposite me I saw my mother wearing Lily's earrings. She was stirring the ajvar and smiling at me, and her mouth smelled sour and reeked of decay. I opened my eyes and saw Jovan standing in front of me. His mouth smelled like my mother's and he was shaking me awake.

# MARTA MARKOSKA

## *The Heights of Felicity*

FELICITY'S FRIENDS TOLD her that even as kids, they'd always imagined when they were grown up and married—although some of them got married at barely seventeen—they'd live by the sea. Strictly speaking, not by the sea—that's just how they described their vivid memory of childhood—rather, near water. Yes, they'd wanted to live wherever there was water. Did they have an inkling they'd grow up to become such vile human beings that they subconsciously associated water with cleansing themselves? Felicity wondered to herself.

For her part, Felicity never aimed very high. She just wanted to get married for love. After that, whether she ended up living in a cabin—even one like Uncle Tom's—or renting in a New Jersey suburb, she didn't even care to think about. In fact, she did aim high, but only on a subconscious level, because she couldn't imagine anything higher than the forty-fifth floor of the only high-rise building in her neighborhood. Yes, she really did aim high, although without being aware of it.

Gordon was her husband. A thirty-eight year old man with dark hair—at least what he had left on his head. Around six feet tall, lean, and muscular. But he wasn't exactly what you'd call model material, because these seemingly ideal features weren't evenly proportioned. As Felicity's grandmother liked to joke about him: "He has a lot of nice features, just not in the right places."

Slightly stooped, and with an aquiline nose—prominent only in profile—Gordon was the type of man that every third woman would put up with. Actually, he's the type that would be bearable, if not for every third woman, then for every fourth, regardless of what she's like as a companion. He was easy to get along with. He didn't grumble much and daily life could go on without any serious obstacles. Felicity's eternal desire for a tall, dark, handsome man at the same time clashed with her desire for him to be reasonably bearable. She told herself that if she could find these two things—for her the most important attributes in a man—she would get married. If not, then she'd buy herself a dog and devote all her love and affection to it. Well, either fate or the cards or luck or quantum physics toying with her, or whatever, led Felicity to Gordon—who was everything but the man of her dreams.

Sometimes to comfort herself, she thought about the lives of her friends. Almost none of them were living their lives the way they wanted to. Jesse, who all her life had preached the importance of being a vegetarian, married a butcher. Linda married Paul, who works in a liquor store, even though she herself had never touched a drop in her life. While Mercy, tormented her whole life by the need for a father figure, had been proposed to by a man eight years her junior, barely out of adolescence. Well, Felicity, things aren't so bad for you after all, she thought to herself, after weighing the pros and cons of her own situation against the fate of those she knew.

Felicity worked as a grocery clerk. At every break, she went outside to spend her few minutes of freedom smoking. She sucked hard on the nicotine to prove to herself that every subsequent drag was deeper than the last one. Her father would be proud of her. When she was a child, they often competed with each other to see who could toss a stone the farthest; whose paper plane would remain in the air the longest; who could stick out their tongue for the longest time in front of the mirror; who could walk the farthest with both feet in one sock. Her mother had left home while she was still sleeping and dreaming of the kind of life she wanted to have when she grew up. Felicity met

Gordon under circumstances almost as competitive as those with her father. One night at the local bar, while playing pool with her friend Kate, some wise guy approached her with a proposal: he would give her one hundred dollars if she was brave enough to give Gordon a passionate kiss without warning. Felicity didn't think twice about it. She grabbed the hundred dollars and threw herself at Gordon while he was waiting in line to go to the bathroom. What harm could there be in an innocent kiss? she thought to herself. She'd earn a hundred dollars and in return make someone happy. To this day, she's not sure whether the guy who gave her the money as a wager wasn't just a friend or acquaintance of Gordon's, who'd given him the hundred dollars to bribe some woman to go up to him. Whatever the case may be, the goal was achieved. Here they are now, still together after eight years. Whenever they fought, Felicity would throw in Gordon's face the fact that, had she not been offered the hundred dollars, she'd never have been with him. He'd just shrug his shoulders. Felicity didn't know whether to interpret this as a sign of indifference, as if he were saying it was all the same to him whether or not they were together, or to take it as a loss for words, a sign of his lack of verbal and intellectual capacity, and of his ignorance of how to deal with attack.

For his part, Gordon didn't consider it worthwhile on any occasion to contradict Felicity, because clearly he loved her more than she did him. He was one of those men who contented himself with buying trinkets from shops with signs that read: EVERYTHING FOR $9.99. And when he found something precious—to him—he felt like a success. As if he'd graduated from Harvard. Then he would shower Felicity with kisses and tenderness, which he didn't do every day, only when he felt like a success. Felicity would fend off these characteristic attempts of his at conquering her neck, ears, head, and even other parts of her body whenever he triumphed in his pursuit of meaningless trinkets. At those times, she too felt meaningless. One day, Gordon came home and said solemnly:

"I bought something I've wanted to have since childhood."

"You bought yourself a dildo?" Felicity interjected sardonically.

"Good grief, Felicity. Where did you get such a silly idea? Do I look like someone who'd buy a dildo?"

Felicity liked to tease Gordon with a bit of dirty talk because she had always found him a bit awkward in bed. She enjoyed these small triumphs, which she set up for her own sweet pleasure.

"Felicity, I bought a silver chain stamped with the name of the inventor of eyeglass chains."

Gordon thought that he'd discovered America every time he found some trinket that in his mind deserved special attention. Yet no one else besides him was familiar with the history, origin, and idea behind that trinket, and even less so with the name of the inventor of such a meaningless object.

"Gordon, with that chain, you could ha—"

She didn't finish her sentence. She wasn't sure he'd get her meaning.

"You would've been better off buying a dildo. And certainly it would be more useful."

Gordon wasn't in the mood for a fight. He didn't take the bait with these kinds of taunts over his awkwardness in bed.

"Gordon, what d'you say you go back to that store and exchange that chain for a dildo? Don't you think that would solve some of our problems?"

Gordon made out as if he hadn't heard what she said. Enthralled by the name on the chain, he immediately ran off to do a Google search to find out whatever information he could about the history of this chain.

"If you feel uncomfortable doing it, then I'll go and exchange that damned chain for a suitable dildo," Felicity said in a slightly raised voice.

"Gordon, if you don't go and exchange that worthless chain, you risk an argument until you do go.

"Gordon, do you hear what I'm saying? If you don't go and exchange that worthless chain right now, I'll throw it over the balcony.

"Gordon, if you don't listen to what I'm saying, I swear that chain with the name of its worthless inventor will end up on the pavement.

"Gordon, I swear that both you and your chain will be thrown from the balcony and you'll make a good example for some inventor—of forensics!"

She grabbed the chain out of his hands, waving it threateningly through the air, and at the moment she tried to throw it as far as she could off the balcony, she tripped on an old candlestick holder that Gordon had bought for $9.99. She had refused to allow such an eyesore—as she referred to it—grace the balcony table, so Gordon had thrown it on the balcony.

Felicity never aimed very high. In fact, she did aim high, but only on a subconscious level, because she couldn't imagine anything higher than the forty-fifth floor of the only high-rise building in her neighborhood. Yes, she really did aim high, although without being aware of it.

# SASHO DIMOSKI

## *Simon*

I WAS . . . I was nowhere. A man with a glow in his eyes. A red glow. A glow that produces spots. Maybe they're lying. They must be lying. Men with glowing eyes. What nonsense. A fabrication. People lie out of fear. There's nothing save fear in lies. Not everyone can bear the truth. Don't make things up. Long ago, long before you existed someone invented the truth. Hence the stains. There's no untruth in blood. A red stain on a white dress. And suddenly even my face becomes red. Small stains. Small stains. That can't be erased. That can't be erased. They remain on the skin. They die here. What dies? Don't ask me what dies when everything is dead. Even my voice is dead. My lips move, that's why you think that I'm speaking. I want to. There's no voice. A hole in my throat. I remember times when I used to sing. Don't laugh. I could slay you with just one song. Not my song. I never wrote even one. But I knew many. Don't laugh. The easiest thing is to be a word. I'm lying. I have words, but I'm nothing. A voice. A word. They have no taste. Color does. It has a red taste. Don't laugh! That's right, a red taste. What kind of taste does your tongue have? What kind of taste does your head have? Something's bursting. Can you hear it? Without a doubt. Yes. It's bursting. Don't laugh. Have you aired out the place? Love is for weaklings. Life is for me. Look: if someone soils your dress, you can shed your skin. Just like that. A person has many skins.

Nine to be precise. Don't ask needless questions. I don't know exactly. I just know that there are nine. I could have killed for his eyes. For his brimful eyes—like a day that contains all the days that have gone by, all the days that are to come. I could have, if I'd wanted to. I should have ripped out his eyes. As he was sleeping. At least one of them. And then turned it to face his other eye. So he could see one eye with his other one, and so he could know that one mustn't invent red stains. This isn't the world. There's nothing. The world died long ago. How did you survive? I didn't see you. An embrace concealed me. It was raining heavily. Pelting down. Then it appeared. An angel. It kissed me. It saved me. It said: You're not for this world. That's why today, I have a white feather on my third skin, right below the red stain on my heart. That's how I fly. You can watch me. Do you want to fly together? That's not possible. The ability to fly is not given to you; it's something you earn. You're a silly man. I could love you. So silly. No. Love has nothing in common with silliness. Something's bursting again. My soul? It burst apart long ago. I saw it, you know. My soul is white as snow. Snow melts. The soul turns to water. That's how they drank me up. Someone swallowed me in one gulp. I didn't stick in even one throat. I rolled down. I felt as though I were inside a stomach. Then in the bowels. And all of a sudden I was outside. That's how the snow becomes dirty. Brown. That's how the snow stinks. Don't talk nonsense. Food for the earth. That's how the grass grows. Green. Then yellow. And then brown. It's that simple. I'll clean up the blood myself. Yes, with a bloodstain remover. You don't know? It's done with tears and hands. The tears are placed on the breast. They're scrubbed. Then, what's left behind on one's hands is washed off with water. The blood is cleaned up with that water. With your own, you know. What kind of nonsense is that? You clean yourself best yourself. There's no greater truth than that. The first time I cried. They took a piece of me. I thought . . . I thought that it was a heart. It wasn't. One woman dies, another is born. Always anew. Every death is new. Every birth is new. My name is empty. My body is filled. My head is crammed. One can die from too many thoughts. It's possible to live with fewer

thoughts. Say something. Say nothing. It makes no difference.
Somebody speaks. Somebody dies. I don't see anything. I flee
death, death flees me. A beautiful woman. No one told you?
My death is a beautiful woman in a white dress spattered with
stains in the form of human faces. The faces are largely stains.
And those stains are overlaid with countless other stains. They
call them sins. I call them blessings. Nobody missed me, that's
why it's a blessing.

Stay, Simon. Don't go anywhere. Don't say anything. Look at
me: this is simply life, there's nothing terrible here. Stay. Make
a pillow of your arm for me. Make a bed of your soul. So I can
dream for you. To be for you what you are for me. Don't say
anything. I will spread out this skin for you. You can put it on if
you're cold. You can erase time with it. Stay. I will be time for you,
and no one will know that the clock has always communicated
silence. I will recount all the great love stories, and you will know
that they were mine purely so I could learn that love lasts as long
as the eyes can see. You shine in my eyes. You shine in my mind.
I bury my fears with these words. I fear only my own desire for
good. The heavens can surpass you in kindness. Everyone can
outdo you. My kindness toward you I call life. Stay. Goodness
comes back with laughter. It will return to you as something
that's awaited. One must take pleasure in the lovely decorations
so that the Christmas tree has meaning. I keep all of your gifts
under my roof. They will never perish. No one will take them.
There's no safer place for your face than this liveliness within me:
when the world calls out your name to me, I know that mine is
being repeated. We have the same name. It suits me well. Like
growing. Into and with the name. One can always choose one's
own name.

Stay. Don't go anywhere. Don't say anything. Look at me:
time stands still when you're not here. Nothing happens. No one
comes. The word grows within me for a whole lifetime. I grow
within myself. Your eyes gave me life.

Don't go off somewhere else with another face in your eyes.
Look at me. Don't leave me. Preserve me the way the drum in
my heart preserves you. With the beats that count down a life.

With footsteps drumming across a swaying bridge—in order to reach the other side of the rainbow. Don't go anywhere without my caresses. Without my time. There'll be no one to safeguard you against the fear in your dream. That's what I'm for. To help you fall asleep when your night has gone off someplace else. So that I can bring you back home—to this room where time begins and ends. Tell me what I'm saying to you. Repeat my heart the way I repeat you with words. I have no voice. You know all my words. Say something. Don't say anything. Don't go without my face. Don't forget me.

Don't go anywhere. Lie down inside me. Dream. I will cover us both with all that I have. This up here. The heavens. All mine. Lie down on my breast. Listen to my heart. Your name is beating inside me. That's how I fall asleep. That's how I wake you. With me for you through the century that lies ahead.

You see.

There'll be another dream for us.

We are such stuff as dreams are made of, you and I. And the stars.

This here is just a small part. Everything is found in a future time. A narrow word.

Stay. It's early yet. The star still hasn't come out on my forehead. That's where you kissed me the first time. That's where I carry you: like a birthmark by which those who know the heavens recognize one another. I know the heavens. It knows me. Look at how it speaks to me, at what it's saying. Don't get up! Listen to me! Listen to me! Only you hear me. Stay. Stay, Simon, stay. I'll call you by whatever name you desire. Choose your own name, just stay. Fine then, perhaps Peter. You can call yourself whatever you like. We'll even invent other stories together. Just stay and listen. I'll tell you all the secrets that I kept to myself. You'll tell me something as well. Only not today. Not today. Simon? Come back. Come back!

# NENAD JOLDESKI

## *My Mother, the Flood, and the Short Story*

One gray September morning, my mother came into my room and woke me up. She wanted to know what kind of stories my father and I swapped. I replied just like any other child: "None, now go away and let me sleep." She was persistent. "They're my stories!" she shouted, "mine, not his!" I looked at her blankly through sleepy eyes. "You work in a bank," I said to her, "perhaps they got mixed up among the account statements." She grew even more excited. She began to talk vaguely about some lost stories and her USB stick, which she apparently found in my father's pocket. Then she went off somewhere. I didn't manage to get back to sleep.

At noon, I had lunch with my father on the outdoor terrace at Café Drim. I didn't mention anything to him about my mother. I just watched him eat. While he ate, he took out a sheet of paper from his pocket. A new story. He said he wanted me to tell him honestly what I thought of it. I smiled. It was called "Flood." I thought about my mother's missing story and I began to read.

FLOOD
I am cleaning and dusting for the umpteenth time. I remove my son's books from the shelves. Before replacing them, and to prevent them from getting damp, I

116

blow gently on the newly wiped surface, the way one blows on coffee to cool it down. I lift the heavy tomes written by Dostoevsky, Chekhov, Borges, Hoffmann, Balzac, Hemingway, the two huge red volumes of Cervantes, Baudelaire . . . Then I begin on the other shelf. A book about Modigliani, several editions of the magazine *Margina*, Kiš, Čačanski, Duracovski, a shabby copy of Rabelais, Eco, and others in no particular order. Seemingly to infinity. How does he find the time to read all of these? I wonder to myself. I finish dusting the shelf and climb onto a chair to wipe the cobwebs that have attached themselves to the corners of his room. I stand on the chair and notice that they're no ordinary spider's webs. I grab a stool and place it on top of the chair. I climb up even higher, just a few inches away from the strange-looking web. I notice that each thread is actually a sentence. But the writing is too small and too closely packed together to read. My glasses don't help either, nor does a magnifying glass. I rise up on my tiptoes as high as I can and maneuver like a clown on a pyramid of chairs. Suddenly I look at the clock above the door and realize that I'm late for work.

I return sometime in the afternoon. The house is empty. I go into my son's room. A surprise awaits me. Now the whole room is filled with sentences spouting from every corner of the ceiling. I imagine myself as a small speck, then I zoom through the scattered strips of text, somehow managing to reach the books. Inside them there is nothing. Just blank pages. All around me, a flood of words. I hear someone enter the house.

My son stares at me harshly. He looks at the scattered sentences and explodes in rage. He grabs his head with both hands and says that all is lost now. He thinks I'm to blame for the mixed up texts. I assure him that everything will be put back in order. He slams the door. I go after him, but he's furious, and has already left the house. Half a sentence dangles from my dress: "Four of us, just like the four corners of the world . . ."

Five hours have passed by and the room is clean. Guided by memory and context, I have returned all the sentences to their respective books. I sit down to write in my diary. I wonder to myself: have I mixed up all the sentences, and if so will my son realize it? I smile and shake off this silly thought. But, it's strange. Deep down, I still feel a nagging doubt gnawing away at me: will he realize it?

"I didn't know that you cleaned and dusted," I said to my father. He just stared at me. Then we both stood up and went off without saying a word. At home we found my mother reading something to my brother. She stopped reading as soon as we came in, and invited us to come and eat. We told her that we weren't hungry. She insisted we eat some of the alphabet soup she'd made. It was definitely the saltiest and bitterest thing I had ever tasted in my life. We ate the excessively salty soup with lowered heads. My mother and my brother kept their eyes on us the whole time.

That evening, I sat down to write about what had happened, but I wasn't sure who it was that was really writing—me or the salt from my mother's soup.

# AUTHOR BIOGRAPHIES

ELIZABETA BAKOVSKA (b. 1969, Bitola) is a prose writer and a poet. She graduated from the Department of English Language and Literature, Faculty of Philology, at the University of Skopje, where she also obtained her MA. She holds a PhD in Gender Studies from the Euro-Balkan Institute in Skopje. She has published three poetry collections: *Biography of Our Love* (2003), *Conditions of Body and Mind After You Turn Thirty* (2005), and *Barbarians Still Write Poetry* (2015); a collection of short stories, *Four Seasons* (2004); one novel, *On The Road to Damascus* (2006); and a book of literary theory and criticism, *A Room of One's Own, a Ghetto of One's Own: Women's Writing in Contemporary Macedonian Prose* (2016). Bakovska is also an editor for *Blesok*, an online journal for literature and other arts.

RUMENA BUŽAROVSKA (b. 1981, Skopje) is one of the leading new voices of contemporary short fiction in Macedonia. She has published three short story collections, including *Scribbles* (2007), *Wisdom Tooth* (2010), and *My Husband* (2014), from which "Lily" is taken, and which is forthcoming with Dalkey Archive Press. "Waves," a story from her second collection, was included in *Best European Fiction 2016*, also published by Dalkey Archive Press. She is a literary translator from English into Macedonian, having translated authors such as Lewis Carroll, J. M. Coetzee, Truman Capote, Charles Bukowski, and Richard Gwyn. She is Assistant Professor of American Literature at the University of Skopje. Her stories have been published in various magazines and anthologies in English, German, Croatian, Serbian, Bulgarian, and French translations, while her short story collection *Wisdom Tooth* was published in Croatia in 2015.

SASHO DIMOSKI (b. 1985, Ohrid) is a poet, playwright, and prose writer. Dimoski is noted for his signature mixing of genres. He has published five books: *Diary of a Hooligan* (2013), a book of experimental prose; the novels *Alma Mahler* (2014) and *The Fifth Season* (2015), both recently published by Dalkey Archive Press; *We, the Others* (2016), a book of collected plays; and *Sleeping Beauties* (2018), his most recent book of experimental prose. Since 2008, Dimoski has been working as a dramatist at Džinot Theatre in Veles. *Alma Mahler*, which was shortlisted for Novel of the Year awarded by daily newspaper *Utrinski Vesnik*, has also been successfully adapted for the stage. Other plays he has written include: *Phaedra* (2015), *Medea* (2016), and *The Assembly Women* (2016). He has also written the librettos *The Red Room* (2017), produced by the Macedonian Opera and Ballet, and *Anna Comnena* (2017) produced by the Džinot Theater, Veles.

NENAD JOLDESKI (b. 1986, Struga) is a short story writer. He has published two short story collections. His debut, *The Silence of Enhalon* (2009), written in a dialect and slang variety of Macedonian, received the Novite Award from Templum Publishing House. His second, *Each with His Own Lake*, was published by Templum in 2012. He was awarded the prestigious European Union Prize for Literature in 2016.

OLIVERA ĆORVEZIROSKA (b. 1965, Kumanovo) is a prose writer, poet, essayist, and literary critic. She has published two poetry collections, *Third Floor* (1982) and *Tall Whites* (1999); five short story collections, *Sorrows of the Young Proofreader* (2000), *(Inter)woven Stories* (2003), for which she won the Stale Popov Award, *Two Pillows* (2010), from which "The Irreplaceable" is taken, *Short Stories without Sugar* (2016), and *Sewn Stories* (2017). She is the author of two novels and a picture book for children. In 2005, she published her first novel for adults, *The Locked Body of Lu*, which was shortlisted for Novel of the Year awarded by daily newspaper *Utrinski Vesnik*. In 2016, "Sugar-Coated City" won Best Short Story awarded by daily newspaper *Nova Makedonija*. Her stories have been translated into numerous languages.

ŽARKO KUJUNDŽISKI (b. 1980, Skopje) is a short story writer, novelist, poet, playwright, editor, and translator. Kujundžiski belongs to the youngest generation of writers in Macedonia. He has published one short story collection, *13* (2010); four novels, including *Spectator* (2003), the first debut novel in the history of contemporary Macedonian literature to have had seven print run editions, *America* (2006), *Found and Lost* (2008), and *Skopje and Everything is Possible* (2013); three plays, *Andrew, Love, and Other Disasters* (2004); three poetry collections, *Susan* (2008), *My Girl Susan Again* (2010), and *We the Items* (2016); stories for children *Tino from my Combo* (2015); and an essay, *The Shortest Long* (2012). His short stories have been translated into numerous languages and have been included in various anthologies in Macedonia and abroad. His short story "When the Glasses are Lost" was included in *Best European Fiction 2013*, published by Dalkey Archive Press. He is owner of Antolog Publishing House and the e-zine Reper. He is also founder of the BookStar Literary Festival.

MITKO MADŽUNKOV (b. 1943, Strumica) is a prose writer, playwright, and essayist. He began his literary career in Belgrade, where he published his first story, "Resurrection," in 1965. He worked at the Belgrade City Library for thirty years, until his retirement. He has won numerous literary awards, including the Isidora Sekulić Award for the short story collection *Kill the Talkative Dog* (1973); the Macedonian Literary Foundation Award for Novel of the Year for *Toward the Other Land* (1993); and Novel of the Year for *The Birds from Last Year's Nest* (2013), awarded by daily newspaper *Utrinski Vesnik*.

KALINA MALESKA (b. 1975, Skopje) is a prose writer, essay-ist, scholar, translator, and editor. She has published three short story collections, *Misunderstandings* (1998), *The Naming of the Insect* (2008), and *Clever Pejo, My Enemy* (2016), from which "The Nonhuman Adversary" is taken; two novels, *Bruno and the Colors* (2006), and *Apparitions with Silver Threads* (2014); and one play, *An Event Among Many* (2010). "A Different Kind of Weapon," a story from her third collection, was included in *Best European Fiction 2018*, published by Dalkey Archive Press. Her stories, as well as her literary essays, have been published in various magazines and journals in Macedonia and abroad. Maleska teaches English Literature in the Faculty of Philology, University of Skopje, where she graduated in English Language and Literature with Comparative Literature, and where she also defended her MA and PhD theses. Maleska also translates liter-ary works from English into Macedonian and vice versa. Some of her translations into Macedonian include *Tristram Shandy* by Laurence Sterne, *Selected Stories* by Ambrose Bierce, and *Huckleberry Finn* by Mark Twain. Maleska is Prose Editor for *Blesok*, an online journal for literature and other arts.

MARTA MARKOSKA (b. 1981, Skopje) is a poet, short story writer, essayist, and multimedia artist. She holds a BA in General and Comparative Literature from the Faculty of Philology, University of Skopje, and a Master's in Cultural Studies in Literature from the Institute of Macedonian Literature in Skopje. She has published eleven books, including the short story col-lection *Whirlpool in Bethlehem* (2010), and the poetry collec-tions *All Tributaries Flow into My Basin* (2009), *Headfirst toward the Heights* (2012), and *Black Holes within Us* (2014). Humor is a common thread that runs through Markoska's prose. Her quirky stories display a sharp wit with a satirical bent. Her work has been translated into various languages and has appeared in numerous anthologies. In 2015, she received the award for Best Short Story from daily newspaper *Nova Makedonija* for "The Heights of Felicity." She is currently working on her new "one-minute-novel" called *Radiant*, and her new book of sensual-erotic poems called *H/ERO/T/IC BOOK*.

JAGODA MIHAJLOVSKA-GEORGIEVA (b. 1953, Skopje) is a short story writer, novelist, and essayist. She is also a journalist, film critic, and TV editor, and has won several awards for Journalist of the Year in print and electronic media. She has published two short story collections, a book of essays, two novels for children, and three novels for adults. She has also written TV travelogues on India, Nepal, and the Himalayas. She has won numerous awards for her short stories, many of which have been translated into other languages and included in various anthologies. She received the prestigious Kočo Racin Prize, Macedonia's highest award for fiction, for her first novel *The Stone of Your Day—Himalayan Story* (2005). She also won Novel of the Year for her second novel, *Indigo Bombay* (2008), awarded by daily newspaper *Utrinski Vesnik*. Her third novel *Monastery Fuenterrabia* was published in 2017.

DRAGI MIHAJLOVSKI (b. 1951, Bitola) is a short story writer, novelist, essayist, scholar, and prolific translator from English to Macedonian and vice versa. He is Professor of the Theory and Practice of Translation and Interpreting at the Faculty of Philology, University of Skopje. He has published nine short story collections and six novels. He is the recipient of numerous awards, including Macedonia's highest award for fiction, the Kočo Racin Prize, for the short story collection *Pole Vault* (1994); he has also twice been awarded the Stale Popov Award for the novels *The Death of the Scrivener* (2002) and *My Scanderbeg* (2006). His works have been translated into numerous languages. His many translations into Macedonian include the complete works of Shakespeare, Milton's *Paradise Lost*, for which he was awarded the Grigor Prličev Prize for Translation in 1995, and *Beowulf*, for which he was awarded the Kiril Pejčinoviќ Prize for Translation in 2010.

BLAŽE MINEVSKI (b. 1961, Gevgelija) is a prose writer, play-wright, and screenwriter. He is the recipient of numerous prestigious national prizes. His short stories and novels have been translated into several languages. Major works include the novels *We Should Have Taken a Photo before We Started Hating Each Other* (1998), *The Story about the Third One* (2003), *The Target* (2007), for which he won several prizes, including Novel of the Year awarded by daily newspaper *Utrinski Vesnik*, and *Me, Tito and Mickey Mouse* (2014). He has published five short story collections, including *The Season of the Dandelions* (2001), for which he won the prestigious Kočo Racin Prize. His short story "Academician Sisoye's Inaugural Speech" was included in *Best European Fiction 2011*, published by Dalkey Archive Press.

SNEŽANA MLADENOVSKA ANGJELKOV (b. 1977, Skopje) is a prose writer and media theorist. She completed her MA in Film and Television at the Faculty of Dramatic Arts in 2012. "Menka" is an extract from her first novel, *Eleven Women* (2011), which won Novel of the Year awarded by daily newspaper *Utrinski Vesnik*. "Beba," also taken from *Eleven Women*, was included in *Best European Fiction 2017*, published by Dalkey Archive Press. She has also published *True-to-Life Pictures* (2014), a theory on film editing and its vital role in shaping creative documentary film with an emphasis on the documentaries of Macedonian director, Vladimir Blaževski. Mladenovska Angjelkov has extensive experience in television editing, and has creatively shaped over five hundred documentaries and travelogues. She is currently working on her second novel.

TOMISLAV OSMANLI (b. 1956, Bitola) is a prolific writer with over twenty books and fifteen screenplays to his name. He is a prose writer, screenwriter, playwright, media theorist, film and theater critic, essayist, and comics enthusiast. His first novel, *The Twenty-First* (2009), was published to critical acclaim, and won Novel of the Year awarded by daily newspaper *Utrinski Vesnik*. The novel has also been published in Croatia, Montenegro, Serbia, Russia, Egypt, and Bulgaria. He has since gone on to publish two further novels: *Behind the Corner* (2012), and *The Ship. A Consarchy* (2016). His works have been translated into numerous languages. He lives in Skopje.

ALEKSANDAR PROKOPIEV (b.1953, Skopje) is a short story writer, essayist, and former member of new wave bands formed in Belgrade and Skopje. He graduated from the Faculty of Philology at the University of Belgrade, and completed his postgraduate education in Belgrade and at the Sorbonne. He has published fourteen books of fiction and essays, including one novella, *The Peeper* (2007). He received the Balkanika Prize 2012 for his short story collection *Homunculus: Fairy Tales for Adults* (2011). His works have been translated into numerous languages. He has also written for film, theater, TV, radio, and comic books. Prokopiev is also the Artistic Director of the Pro-Za Balkan International Festival of Literature, Skopje, Macedonia.

BERT STEIN is the pen name of BRANKO PRLJA (b. 1977, Sarajevo, Bosnia-Herzegovina). He has been living in Skopje since 1990. He is a prose writer and translator. He has published twenty books, including short story collections, novels, experimental prose, and children's books. He is founder of Electrolit, the first ever award competition for e-stories in Macedonia. He has a BA in Graphic Design, and has worked as an art director and copywriter in various publishing and advertising houses. He is also founder and editor-in-chief of the art collective KAPKA (Creative Activism through Parody, Criticism, and Allegory). "Seventh Son of a Seventh Son" is an extract from his novel *Three Minutes and Fifty-three Seconds* (2015), which was shortlisted for Novel of the Year awarded by daily newspaper *Utrinski Vesnik*. More information about the author and his work: kapka.com.mk

# RIGHTS AND PERMISSIONS

# Selected Dalkey Archive Paperbacks

Michal Ajvaz, *Empty Streets*
  *Journey to the South*
  *The Golden Age*
  *The Other City*
David Albahari, *Gotz & Meyer*
  *Learning Cyrillic*
Pierre Albert-Birot, *The First Book of Grabinoulor*
Svetlana Alexievich, *Voices from Chernobyl*
Felipe Alfau, *Chromos*
  *Locos*
João Almino, *Enigmas of Spring*
  *Free City*
  *The Book of Emotions*
Ivan Ângelo, *The Celebration*
David Antin, *Talking*
Djuna Barnes, *Ladies Almanack*
  *Ryder*
John Barth, *The End of the Road*
  *The Floating Opera*
  *The Tidewater Tales*
Donald Barthelme, *Paradise*
  *The King*
Svetislav Basara, *Chinese Letter*
  *Fata Morgana*
  *The Mongolian Travel Guide*
Andrej Blatnik, *Law of Desire*
  *You Do Understand*
Patrick Bolshauser, *Rapids*
Louis Paul Boon, *Chapel Road*
  *My Little War*
  *Summer in Termuren*
Roger Boylan, *Killoyle*
Ignacio de Loyola Brandão, *And Still the Earth*
  *Anonymous Celebrity*
  *The Good-Bye Angel*
Sébastien Brebel, *Francis Bacon's Armchair*
Christine Brooke-Rose, *Amalgamemnon*
Brigid Brophy, *In Transit*
  *Prancing Novelist: In Praise of Ronald Firbank*
Gerald L. Bruns, *Modern Poetry and the Idea of Language*
Lasha Bugadze, *The Literature Express*
Dror Burstein, *Kin*
Michel Butor, *Mobile*
Julieta Campos, *The Fear of Losing Eurydice*
Anne Carson, *Eros the Bittersweet*
Camilo José Cela, *Family of Pascual Duarte*
Louis-Ferdinand Céline, *Castle to Castle*
Hugo Charteris, *The Tide Is Right*
Luis Chitarroni, *The No Variations*
Jack Cox, *Dodge Rose*
Ralph Cusack, *Cadenza*
Stanley Crawford, *Log of the S.S. the Mrs. Unguentine*
  *Some Instructions to My Wife*
Robert Creeley, *Collected Prose*
Nicholas Delbanco, *Sherbrookes*
Rikki Ducornet, *The Complete Butcher's Tales*
William Eastlake, *Castle Keep*
Stanley Elkin, *The Dick Gibson Show*
  *The Magic Kingdom*
Gustave Flaubert, *Bouvard et Pécuchet*
Jon Fosse, *Melancholy I*
  *Melancholy II*
  *Trilogy*
Max Frisch, *I'm Not Stiller*
  *Man in the Holocene*
Carlos Fuentes, *Christopher Unborn*
  *Great Latin American Novel*
  *Nietzsche on His Balcony*
  *Terra Nostra*
  *Where the Air Is Clear*
William Gaddis, *J R*
  *The Recognitions*

William H. Gass, *A Temple of Texts*
  *Cartesian Sonata and Other Novellas*
  *Finding a Form*
  *Life Sentences*
  *Reading Rilke*
  *Tests of Time: Essays*
  *The Tunnel*
  *Willie Masters' Lonesome Wife*
  *World Within the Word*
Etienne Gilson, *Forms and Substances in the Arts*
  *The Arts of the Beautiful*
Douglas Glover, *Bad News of the Heart*
Paulo Emílio Sales Gomes, *P's Three Women*
Juan Goytisolo, *Count Julian*
  *Juan the Landless*
  *Marks of Identity*
Alasdair Gray, *Poor Things*
Jack Green, *Fire the Bastards!*
Jiří Gruša, *The Questionnaire*
Mela Hartwig, *Am I a Redundant Human Being?*
John Hawkes, *The Passion Artist*
Dermot Healy, *Fighting with Shadows*
  *The Collected Short Stories*
Aidan Higgins, *A Bestiary*
  *Bornholm Night-Ferry*
  *Langrishe, Go Down*
  *Scenes from a Receding Past*
Aldous Huxley, *Point Counter Point*
  *Those Barren Leaves*
  *Time Must Have a Stop*
Drago Jančar, *The Galley Slave*
  *I Saw Her That Night*
  *The Tree with No Name*
Gert Jonke, *Awakening to the Great Sleep War*
  *Geometric Regional Novel*
  *Homage to Czerny*
  *The Distant Sound*
  *The System of Vienna*
Guillermo Cabrera Infante, *Infante's Inferno*
  *Three Trapped Tigers*
Jacques Jouet, *Mountain R*
Mieko Kanai, *The Word Book*
Yorum Kaniuk, *Life on Sandpaper*
Ignacy Karpowicz, *Gestures*
Pablo Katchadjian, *What to Do*
Hugh Kenner, *The Counterfeiters*
  *Flaubert, Joyce, and Beckett: The Stoic Comedia*
  *Gnomon*
  *Joyce's Voices*
Danilo Kiš, *A Tomb for Boris Davidovich*
  *Garden, Ashes*
Pierre Klossowski, *Roberte Ce Soir and The Revocatio of the Edict of Nantes*
George Konrád, *The City Builder*
Tadeusz Konwicki, *The Polish Complex*
Elaine Kraf, *The Princess of 72nd Street*
Édouard Levé, *Suicide*
Mario Levi, *Istanbul Was a Fairytale*
Deborah Levy, *Billy & Girl*
José Lezama Lima, *Paradiso*
Osman Lins, *Avalovara*
António Lobo Antunes, *Knowledge of Hell*
  *The Splendor of Portugal*
Mina Loy, *Stories and Essays of Mina Loy*
Joaquim Maria Machado de Assis, *Collected Stories*
Alf Maclochlainn, *Out of Focus*
Ford Madox Ford, *The March of Literature*
D. Keith Mano, *Take Five*
Micheline Marcom, *A Brief History of Yes*
  *The Mirror in the Well*
Ben Marcus, *The Age of Wire and String*
Wallace Markfield, *Teitlebaum's Widow*
  *To an Early Grave*
David Markson, *Reader's Block*
  *Wittgenstein's Mistress*
Carole Maso, *AVA*